JULIE

JULIE

Cora Taylor

CANONGATE · KELPIES

First published in Canada in 1985
by Western Producer Prairie Books, Saskatoon
First published in Great Britain in 1988
by Spindlewood
First published by Canongate Kelpies in 1990
Second impression 1990

© 1985 Cora Taylor

Cover illustration by Alexa Rutherford

Printed and bound in Great Britain
by Cox and Wyman Ltd, Reading

ISBN 0 86241 290 0

CANONGATE PUBLISHING LTD
16 FREDERICK STREET, EDINBURGH EH2 2HB

To my mother, Edith Mary Traub,
Who always thought I would,
And my husband, Russ Taylor,
Who always said I could.

CHAPTER ONE

She could see them. The sails ballooning, coming across the field with a smooth silent motion, rising and falling like a giant horse galloping. Only slowly. Tall ships with rows and rows of full, fat sails tossed as though the black summer-fallow field were ridged with waves and not furrows. Then they were gone and all Julie could see were the sheets on the clothesline over by the house, the bottoms caught on the barbed wire fence, straining to hold the summer wind. The beautiful ships were gone but she had seen them. She had.

She wished she could tell someone. Run home, or stop Charlie, on the tractor, ploughing in the next field.

'The ships, didn't you see them? They went right by you.' And she could tell him how beautiful they were. How the biggest one had sails like three rows of sheets caught on the fence, each row larger than the one above, and how it was taller than the old balm o'Gilead by the barn. And the other ships, all of them different, their swollen sails different too, and all of them moving without a sound.

It was hard to keep it to herself but she knew the way Charlie would stare at her, then laugh and shake his head. She would keep quiet but it was hard. And lonely.

People who met the ten-year-old Julie for the first time noticed her silence and nodded wisely saying, 'Takes after her dad that one. Will always was the quiet type.'

It was true. When company came they both hid out. He would find something urgently in need of fixing in the workshop, if he hadn't time or excuse to be out in the fields, and Julie would slip away to play by herself in the trees back of the garden or in the willow stand in the sheep pasture. If she was caught indoors she'd find a quiet spot upstairs and stay there until everyone left. Once, when she was five, she did not reappear and the frantic family searched everywhere, finding her at last, asleep under her sisters' double bed.

The shy one, people said. But her family knew this wasn't so.

Julie had been different from the beginning. Small and dark after six strapping towheads, her father called her his 'little Celtic throwback' and her mother laughed and said she was a 'sweet wee changeling child'. Perhaps this was why after solid names like Charlie, Mary, Jimmy, Joe, Jane, and Billy, the last little Morgan was christened Juliet.

She had been different then, but it was not her silent shyness that made her so, instead it was her awareness and joy of discovery that set her apart. No baby Morgan ever laughed and crowed with Julie's enthusiasm.

And talk. Julie learned younger than any of the others. It seemed as though she never went through the one-word-at-a-time hesitation, but gushed sentences from the very beginning, like a dam bursting.

'Julie's better than television,' Mary said, high praise since the Morgans didn't have a set then and Mary was able to watch it only when she was visiting friends. 'She gets so excited and describes everything just as though it was right there. Sometimes I turn around and look. You start to believe it's real she tells it so well.'

Julie's imagination was a source of amazement for her brothers and sisters and amusement for her parents.

'Out in the field, big hairy aminals are running very fast. There are lots and lots of them. If you aren't careful they will run over you.' Julie's eyes were wide and seemed to grow even darker.

'How big are they?' Mary prompted.

'Big and big.' Julie stood on the chair reaching as high as she could. 'As big as Bally.' Bally was the Morgan's Simmental bull. 'But they aren't nice and smooth like Bally. They're brown and some have coats like Mr Goodwin's.'

Mr Goodwin had been a member of the Winnipeg police force and had managed somehow to keep the traditional buffalo coat. Those people around the town of Hurry who liked him maintained that he had been given it as a reward for service — something like a retiring teacher's bell. His detractors claimed it was kept without the approval or knowledge of the Winnipeg Police Department.

'Hey, Mum, Julie's telling the kids about a buffalo stampede. How's she know about that?' Charlie, nearly fourteen, didn't listen to Julie's stories as much as the others; his mother, who had Julie's chattering to listen to all day, found the evenings when the older children played with her a relief. She realized she hadn't heard a 'Julie tale', as Mary called them, for a long time.

She dried her hands on her apron. 'Nonsense, Charlie, she's only three. She's certainly never seen a buffalo. She doesn't even know the word.'

'She doesn't call them buffalo. She says they're "big aminals". Come on . . . listen.'

They stood in the doorway listening as Julie told her audience how the big animals ran. 'They go so fast and there's so many of them that they make thunder in the ground when they run.' Julie loved the prairie thunderstorms. She would watch them, eyes shining, and tell the others what was happening in the sky world.

'Why are the big animals running, Julie?' Jane asked.

'I don't know. Maybe they're cold. They only have Mr Goodwin's coat on their shoulders, then they're bare . . . nearly.' Julie laughed. 'They're funny. Funny looking aminals.'

'See, Mum,' Charlie whispered, 'she's talking about buffalo all right.'

'Maybe something's chasing them?' Billy, at five, was the closest to Julie in age: a quiet, stolid little boy who seemed untouched by any imagination of his own. He was his little sister's biggest fan.

Julie stopped laughing and looked puzzled, then frightened. 'Yes that's right. People are chasing them, running from a long way, from all directions.'

'On horseback?'

'No, running. Lots of them.' Julie's face crumbled. 'The aminals can't stop! They'll fall in the ravine. No! Stop! They're falling. No! No!' Julie's cries became sobs.

'It's okay, Julie. Don't cry.' Mary held her, rocking gently. 'It's all right now.' Mary smiled across at her mother. 'Boy, what an imagination this kid has.'

'How could that be imagination, Will?' her mother asked the next morning. 'Don't things children imagine have to be based on something they've seen or heard about? Even if she'd seen a picture of buffalo, how could she describe a stampede so well?'

'Beats me, Alice.' He took his jacket off the hook behind the kitchen door. 'You say she described these animals perfectly last night? Could be that she saw us chasing the cattle out there yesterday trying to sort out Behan's yearling steer. They were doing a lot of running.' He finished buttoning his coat and opened the door before he turned to her again. 'Funny thing, Old Man Behan told me yesterday his dad used

11

to tell him there was a buffalo jump around here — claimed he and his brother dug around at the bottom for bones when they were kids.'

'Where?' Her voice was sharp, almost frightened.

He smiled uneasily. 'Out back here in our ravine. Don't worry, maybe Julie heard about it.' There was little conviction in his voice. 'I'm going into town this afternoon. That part I ordered for the combine is in. You might as well come along and get your groceries today and save another trip.'

Alice Morgan stood thinking for several minutes after the door closed, then sighed, poured a cup of coffee, and sat down to compose her grocery list. It took more time than usual. Between entries she paused much longer than necessary. 'Pick. salt,' she wrote, staring out the window at the empty pasture; 'liq. Certo.' She shook her head slowly. As she wrote 'brn. sgr.' she remembered the large, frightened eyes of her daughter.

How did buffalo fall? she wondered. End over end? She remembered a Tarzan movie she'd seen as a child. Pursued by a rogue elephant, Tarzan came to the edge of a cliff, seized a convenient vine, and swung over the precipice while his pursuer toppled over and over, spiralling down to its death. Like that? Or did they drop straight down spread-eagled? Or head first? Right side up? How? It was unsettling to think that Julie might know.

Later, Julie, still sleepy from her nap, looked out of the window as her mother brushed her tousled curls.

'Look, Mummy,' she pointed to the lawn where the fallen leaves eddied about under the trees, still bright with colour in the afternoon sun, 'dancers.'

Yesterday her mother would have felt a thrill of pleasure because Julie had noticed beauty and made such a sensitive comparison. Now she felt disturbed.

'Leaves,' she said, lifting Julie down from the chair.

'But, Mummy, didn't you see? I liked the little lady in red. Couldn't she jump and turn?'

Alice Morgan realized that her response in the past had always been agreement. She had never challenged Julie's descriptions, had thought them sensitive ... picturesque. 'Yes dear, they are beautiful,' she would have said and they would have stood in pleasant silence, watching. The morning's uneasiness returned.

She felt she had to confront Julie but she hated it.

'I see beautiful coloured leaves, Julie,' she said evenly, 'and the wind is pushing them around.'

'But, Mummy,' Julie's dark eyes were puzzled by this contradiction, 'they have arms and legs and they're dancing on their toes.'

'They look lovely, like dancers, Julie, but they are leaves.'

Alice Morgan's voice was sharpened by her fear.

Something was going wrong and she couldn't stop it or pretend it wasn't there.

'But, Mummy . . .' Julie's lip trembled.

'No, Julie. I don't want to hear any more about it.' I've probably never spoken in anger to her before, Alice thought, as she watched Julie run out sobbing. I hate this, but I've got to start now. She must recognize what's true and what's imagination.

Dancers . . . and not the kind she's seen at the one dance in Hurry that she's been to with the local people: adults dressed up in clothes that hadn't lost their newness, teenaged girls in their usual blue jeans but with eyes exotic with mascara, and grandparents smiling and chatting with their friends, and dancing the occasional waltz. The dancing the teens did might have some turning in it but it was jerky and there was no jumping. And there was certainly no dancing on the toes. She thought of the stomping good humour of the butterfly or the schottische and shook her head. Where had Julie seen ballet? Pictures, naturally. But where?

She could see Will bring the truck around to the front and she picked up her list and purse, tidying up the pile of magazines on the bench behind the table as she did so. There it was — the Christmas catalogue. Why did they send it in September? By the time you wanted to order anything it was in tatters, the children had it so dog-eared and marked up. 'Mum, if I can have this I don't want anything else.' Of course, next week it was a different item.

14

There it was. She noticed an item circled and marked 'for Mary, PLEASE.' Item 3b — a jewellery box that played when you opened it. There, in the centre, a ballerina standing on her toes. Of course, that's where Julie had seen a 'dancer.'

She moved quickly out to the truck. Beside the step a bright red leaf seemed to spin a little faster than the others. It was not at all like the stiff plastic ballerina in the music box.

Julie was already sitting in the truck beside her father, small and solemn on the seat. All the way into town she seemed to be thinking very hard.

Her mother watched her, wanting very much to hold her and say, 'I'm sorry I was cross with you.' But she was afraid to — afraid to risk a return to the topic of leaves that were dancers.

A restraint grew between them from that day. They seemed to be watchful. Julie was so careful with her mother. Always wary. 'Is that all right, Mummy?' she would keep asking whenever she said something, as if she were never sure what her mother's reaction would be.

Alice Morgan found herself gazing sadly at her daughter wondering why she felt guilty. After all she had been right. They were leaves, not dancers, and Julie had to learn to distinguish between truth and fantasy. It hurt though, to have her baby treating her as though she was a stranger in the house who had to be figured out and placated. An unreasonable, unpredictable stranger.

Still, Julie remained as affectionate as ever —

running to her mother at odd moments for a hug and kiss — and gradually some of the tension relaxed. Things could never be the same, but then they never are as children grow up.

At least the uneasiness was gone. Some of it.

CHAPTER TWO

Slowly Julie learned not to trust her audience. One by one she lost them, and she lost Billy last of all.

It was in the wintertime. She was four. Jane and Billy still liked to listen to 'Julie tales' and even Joe, who was almost ten, stuck around to hear one now and then. As he told Jimmy, the kid was interesting at times.

Tonight it had started as usual with someone prompting her.

'Tell us more about the lady, Julie.' Jane plumped up the cushions on the couch and made herself comfortable.

Julie climbed up beside her and squeezed her eyes tight shut. She always started that way.

'She lived long ago and far away.'

Billy sighed contentedly and snuggled into the sheepskin in front of the Franklin stove. Julie never began her stories with 'Once upon a time' like Mum used to but Billy thought these were just as good. 'Long ago and far away' meant the same thing as far as he was concerned.

'It was different then. People lived in the woods. Sometimes there were a few houses together.'

'Like Hurry?' Jane prompted.

Julie looked puzzled. 'Not like Hurry. It was . . . different.'

'How?' Jane was persistent.

'Different.' Julie looked confused and unhappy.

'Never mind, Jane. Just let Julie tell the story.' Billy was patient. He'd noticed that you had to be careful not to be too specific. He could tell that Julie wasn't sure about some things in her stories — mostly how to fit them into anything that went on here and now. You had to keep her in the long ago and far away part or she seemed to get all mixed up and upset.

'Remember, Julie,' Billy prompted, 'last time you told us about the lady and the magic tree.'

Julie shook her head. 'Not magic.'

Billy could have kicked himself. Here he was, upset with the others for mixing her up and now he was doing it. The tree, he remembered, had some special power or something but he could see 'magic' was the wrong word.

'No,' said Jane. 'The tree where the people went to dance. Right, Julie?'

Julie nodded, then looked at them suspiciously. 'They were people dancing, not leaves.'

'Of course not,' laughed Jane. 'They were people dancing around the tree.'

Billy could see Julie relax a little. She would be able to tell the story now. He waited.

'The lady is not happy any more,' Julie said, her eyes shut tight again. This time nobody interrupted. 'There are bad people in the country now. They are big and mean and the little people have to hide. But they don't hide all the time. Sometimes the bad people see them but not often.'

Julie opened her eyes now and looked at them. 'Not all of the big people are bad, so sometimes the lady doesn't hide. Then one day, she makes a mistake. Well, not really a mistake, because at first the people she meets are only surprised and a little scared. But then she knows that they are thinking about hurting her. At first they are smiling at her and she doesn't see what is in their heads until it's too late — too late to hide and so she runs. But they chase her and chase her so she runs to the tree and it takes her inside.'

'Inside?'

Julie had her eyes shut again and did not seem to hear Joe's question. 'The bad people look everywhere, but they can't find her.'

'You mean it's an old hollow tree? I thought you said it was a big green tree with big leaves and vines with white berries on it.' Jane persisted.

Julie opened her eyes. Billy could tell she was unsure of what to say. He wished Jane would just shutup and listen instead of always trying to pin Julie down.

'It is.' Julie's voice was positive.

'So how does the lady hide in it?' Now Joe is asking.

'The tree takes her inside it, like . . . like a stone in a peach.'

'And then what happens?' Billy prompted. He just wanted to get Julie back on the track of the story.

'The bad people are really afraid and they go away, but whenever they pass through the forest they are afraid of the tree because they know the tree is not an ordinary tree and they know something happened to the lady there.' Julie finished and opened her eyes.

'Is that the end?' asked Joe.

Dumb question, Billy thought. Trust Joe to ask a dumb question like that. He should know by now that there was no 'and they lived happily ever after' in Julie's stories. In fact they usually didn't end at all. Just kept on like rivers and birthdays and everything else in the world.

'So does the lady climb out of the tree and go home or what?' asked Jane.

'She can't. She has to stay there.'

'Julie, you do beat everything! How do you think these things up?' Jane jumped up and headed for the door.

'I didn't think it up. She is part of the tree and that is how . . . that is how come some trees are different.'

'Julie old kid, you're weird sometimes,' Joe shook his head. 'Mum's going to have to sort you out if you believe all that stuff.'

Julie looked stricken and Billy, as usual, came to her defence. 'Lay off, you guys. Quit picking on Julie! Just because you —'

'Why don't you little kids go to bed. It's past your bedtime!' With that parting shot Jane and Joe presented a united front in the shape of two backs going out the door.

Billy waited until he was sure Joe couldn't hear him and finished, 'Just because you two turkeys couldn't make up a story in a million years.'

Julie smiled at him. 'Thank you, Billy. You are the very best good brother in the world!'

Billy felt good. Probably, he thought, he felt like the 'very best good brother in the world.' It was a great feeling.

Julie came over and gave him a hug. 'I won't tell them any more stories,' she said sadly. 'Oh Billy! I'm so glad I've still got you!'

It was only a matter of weeks before she lost him.

Billy took the responsibility of being 'the very best good brother in the world' seriously, and he worried about Julie. Now that she felt she couldn't tell anyone but Billy her stories, it seemed to him that they got stranger and stranger. Not that he minded fairy tales that much, but Julie had this way of acting as if they were all true, even if they had happened 'long ago and far away.' The story of the lady and the tree had gone on and on and now there were soldiers with swords and the soldiers had cut down the tree. According to Julie, that had not only killed the tree but the lady as well. He noticed tears welling in Julie's eyes.

'Julie, for Pete's sake, if you don't like sad endings, change it. Make it a happy story.'

She was snuggling down in her bottom bunk under the big old quilt. 'I can't change the story. That's how it was.'

'Well then, make up a happy story instead.'

'But I don't make them up.'

Billy sighed. He'd done it again. 'I mean,' he said carefully, 'how do you know all those stories you tell?'

The answer took her quite a while. 'I hear them,' she said at last.

Billy had a nasty feeling in his stomach. He wished he hadn't asked but it was too late now. 'Do Mum or Mary read them to you? I don't ever remember hearing them.'

'I hear them at night. The lady tells them.' Julie's voice sounded very small and far away.

Relief made Billy's voice loud even to his own ears. 'Oh, you mean you dream them? They're just dreams that you remember afterwards?' He was so relieved that he almost didn't hear Julie's answer. Almost.

'No. I'm not asleep when the lady comes. She comes when I wake up sometimes in the night. And she tells me those stories and lots of other stories too.'

Oh boy, thought Billy, this is worse than I figured. 'Julie, you're just dreaming. The lady is a dream. There is no lady.'

There was a warning in his voice, but Julie missed it. 'She's real, Billy. I know it's not a dream.'

'Stop it, Julie! Everybody's going to make fun of you if you keep saying things like that and act like you believe them. They'll think you're not normal.'

'But it's true, Billy. I know it's true.' Julie was

22

sobbing. Louder and louder. Like no crying Billy had ever heard before. Like a child who has lost everything and is all alone in the world. He relented. 'Aw, Julie, you're still a nice little sister but you gotta learn to tell the difference between stories and dreams and what is real and true.'

It didn't help. Julie couldn't stop. She cried. Deep racking sobs until the door opened and their father came in, picked her up, and held her.

Billy pretended to be asleep.

'What's the matter, little one? Have a bad dream?' Will Morgan's big, work-hard hand was gentle on Julie's hair. The word 'dream' brought on fresh crying.

Alice's voice came up the stairs. 'Is she all right?'

Will wrapped Julie's quilt around her and carried her out before he replied. 'She'll be fine. Won't you, honey? C'mon, we'll rock a bit.'

Julie liked the old rocker in her parents' bedroom. Will would tell her how his Granny Morgan had rocked him in it when he was a little boy. Sometimes he would tell Julie about her. She was Welsh and had lived near Camelot when she was a little girl. She believed in King Arthur, he said.

This time he didn't talk until Julie's sobs quieted, until all that was left were hiccoughs.

'Do you want me to tell you a story, Julie?' he asked.

The word 'story' almost made her start crying again but she held it to a sob and buried her face in the quilt. She knew her father didn't tell stories, he just rambled on about when he was a little boy, about comfortable things. Julie nodded.

'Now would you believe it, Julie, this here quilt's not only older than you are but it's older than I am and parts of it were around long before even my mother was born.'

'But your mum made it.' Julie remembered her mother telling her it was what was called a 'memory quilt.' Not the kind of quilt with a fancy pattern like Log Cabin or Star of Bethlehem that brides long ago made for their trousseaus, but the kind a busy pioneer mother stitched together with patches of all sizes forming no pattern, just because she needed another cover to keep her family warm.

'That's right, she did. But in those days people saved everything. If a dress or shirt or pair of pants got too small or had a hole that couldn't be patched, mothers would just take it apart and make something else from the material. Any pieces left over went into the quilt bag and next time she made a quilt she'd just patch together all those bits of cloth. Of course, if she was making something out of new material, there'd be patches left over when she cut out the pattern and those would go in too. That's why they're called "patchwork" quilts.'

'Mum says this one's called a "memory" quilt.'

He smiled. 'I suppose she's right. When you look at each piece of cloth you can remember the clothing that matched it and that reminds

24

you of what you were doing when you wore it.'

'Can you remember any of these?'

'Hmmm.' He held the old quilt up to the light. 'Can't say as I recognize many of them.' He pointed to a soft brown and blue flannel rectangle, 'I think that came from a shirt of my dad's — at least he had one like it when I was little. And this one . . . feel this one Julie. Rough, isn't it?'

It was a heavy blue material, not at all soft, almost like sandpaper on Julie's cheek.

'That was from my father's wedding suit and he wore it for years. He called it his "Sunday-go-to-Meetin'" suit. Then finally my mother made it over for me. That material's called serge and it wore like iron. Nearly took the hide off me. I wore my long johns every Sunday, even in summer, whenever I wore that suit just so's I wouldn't have that stuff next to my skin.'

Julie smiled. She could see that boy, scrubbed and polished and itching in his church pew.

'This piece I remember too. It's called gingham and my mother had a blouse made out of it. I always thought she looked specially nice when she wore it. The colour matched her eyes. She had blue eyes just like Jane's. You and I got Granny Morgan's eyes.'

'I like this piece best.' Julie smoothed a square that contrasted with the other dark patches. It was dark too — a rich royal blue — but even though it had lost some of its lustre, the quality

25

of the satin still made it soft and the smoothness of it lingered on Julie's fingers and made them tingle.

'That started out as my Granny Morgan's wedding gown. She brought it with her when she came to Canada as a young woman. Saved it for years in the cedar chest and then one day when my mother needed a dress for the Christmas concert and dance at our school — it was a special occasion because I was giving my first recitation —'

'Your first time? Were you scared?'

'You bet I was, but I didn't notice because Granny Morgan made that old wedding gown into a dress and mine was the prettiest mother there. Granny Morgan told me to look at my mum and I wouldn't be scared and forget the words, and it worked. I'd never seen a lady dressed so fine.'

'And you felt brave and special because she was your mother?'

He nodded. 'Not only that but once I looked away and forgot the words. Couldn't remember a thing until I looked back at my mother and there were the words clear as a bell in my head. Afterward I looked at Granny Morgan and she was clapping and smiling up at me just like she'd done it all.'

Julie closed her eyes and held the quilt patch to her face. She could see a young woman in a full dress with strange puffy sleeves. She could see other people dressed in strange long dresses and men in funny suits, and she wanted to see a little boy in an itchy blue serge suit but he didn't seem to be there.

She noticed that the lady was carrying flowers and it was springtime outside and the smiling eyes were brown, not blue. And then Julie recognized her. The lady who came at night and told her the stories was Granny Morgan. She was still smiling when Julie fell asleep and her father carried her back to her bed and tucked the old quilt carefully around her.

Next morning Julie pretended to be sleeping when her mother called Billy for breakfast. She burrowed into the pillow and pulled the quilt over her head to drown out the clatter and scramble of a school-day morning.

When the final door slam heralded the departure of Joe, always the last Morgan to run for the school bus, Alice came in to Julie.

Julie lay very still, remembering not to squeeze her eyes tight shut but just to keep them still.

'Good morning, Julie. I've brought you some juice. You needn't pretend to be asleep.'

Julie's eyes snapped open. 'You knew? But I was being careful.' Perhaps her mother was different too.

'Your eyelids were fluttering,' said Alice matter-of-factly, straightening the covers. 'Up you get. There's work to do and we're going visiting this afternoon. You've never been to visit Granny Goderich have you?'

'Is she my real Granny, like Granny Morgan?'

'No. She's nobody's granny really. And the

27

Granny Morgan that your dad talks about all the time was your great-grandmother. I suppose the closest thing you've got to a real grandmother is my Aunt Em and you've hardly seen her. Hurry and get dressed now.'

Julie was already up and half under the bed looking for her socks.

CHAPTER THREE

The geraniums stood two deep on the window sills. They crowded the stands in front of the windows, spilled onto the sewing machine, and covered an old trunk in the front hall of Granny Goderich's house. Their musty, dusty odour filled the room. The smell caught in Julie's nose just as the dust caught in the fuzzy geranium leaves.

Julie sat very still watching the winter sun glint off Granny Goderich's glasses making her look as if she had large, shining eyes. Even Granny Goderich smelled of geraniums. She wore a fuzzy green flannel dress the colour of geranium leaves.

'So this is your sweet wee changeling child, Alice.'

Alice Morgan set her teacup down with a clatter. She visited the old Goderich home only once a year — the old lady made her nervous. If there was trouble at home, money problems or even a tiff with Will, Granny Goderich always seemed to sense it and ask a question Alice didn't want to answer. She'd chosen to come today because things were going well and she'd felt . . . well . . . safe. Not that Granny Goderich was unkind or a gossip — she kept the things she learned to herself — it was just that Alice didn't like talking about problems too much. It made them grow, she thought.

'How old are you now, Julie?'

'Four,' said Julie looking straight at the shining eyes. 'Almost five.'

'The last one at home,' Alice broke in. 'It seems strange not having a flock of them around. Of course the minute the school bus comes it's bedlam.' She laughed, wishing her voice didn't sound so shrill, her laugh so nervous.

Granny Goderich sighed. 'It's always special with the last little bird that leaves the nest. I remember my George . . .' The old woman's voice trailed off and she stirred her tea in sad silence.

Julie moved over to stand in front of the old sideboard. It was cluttered with interesting old dishes and ornaments. A pink china lady whose china skirt whipped daringly about her ankles, blown by some invisible wind, stood on the bracket right by Julie's nose but she stared instead at a squat purple jar on the topmost shelf of the sideboard. On either side of the jar were pottery dogs: scotties, cocker spaniels, a Saint Bernard with a cask around its neck, a liver-coloured retriever with Souvenir of Saskatoon written on it in white letters, a dalmatian with one leg missing; and a poorly carved wooden puppy; but Julie looked only at the jar.

Alice felt uncomfortable. The loss of George Goderich had been the one sorrow the old lady had never been able to overcome. George was nine years old when he had been killed in a train accident while visiting his grandparents in eastern Canada.

'I didn't want him to go, you know. I told my husband not to take him on that trip.' Her voice was almost keening. 'I knew he shouldn't go, but I didn't insist. I was too weak. I let him go.'

The silence hung awkwardly in the room. More to break it than as a remonstrance, for Julie was a well-behaved child, Alice said, 'Don't touch anything, dear.'

Julie was still standing staring at the purple jar. Her hands were behind her back, not touching anything. Her mother noticed with a start that Julie's face was wet with tears.

'Why, Julie, whatever is wrong?'

Julie didn't answer, instead Granny Goderich answered for her. 'She sees George's ashes, don't you dear?' The grey head turned slowly. 'Alice, did you know Julie was a sensitive child?'

It was one of those questions Alice did not want to answer. She knew what Granny Goderich meant by 'sensitive'. It was not what most people meant. Her mind was still coping with the fact that here, in this living room, amongst the bric-a-brac on the sideboard, this lonely old woman kept the ashes of a son who had died over fifty years ago. And nobody knew about it. Alice was sure of that. It would have been district gossip if they had. So how did Julie know? It wasn't an urn, not the kind crematoriums use, and Julie wouldn't recognize one anyway. It looked very much like an old ginger jar. Alice wanted to get up and run out. She realized that Granny Goderich was no longer waiting for an answer to her question but had gone to Julie, dried her eyes, and given her a biscuit from a tin

31

cookie box with a picture of the Queen at Balmoral on the top.

'Would you like more tea, Alice?'

'No . . . no, thank you. It's getting on. We really can't stay too long.'

'Well then,' Granny Goderich's voice was brisk, normal again. 'I'll read your teacup before you go.' She reached out for it.

'Not today . . . please.' Alice wished she didn't seem so nervous. She shouldn't have blurted her refusal so sharply. Granny read everyone's teacup. She had a reputation for accuracy. Alice had always thought it was just the result of all the shrewd questioning that went with the drinking of the tea. Reading tea leaves was just Granny Goderich's way of giving advice. Good advice too because she was a wise old woman. Some people came every week for tea with Granny. 'She's better than a psychiatrist and the tea is free,' Will said. Still, Alice didn't want her teacup read. Not today. Not with the sight of Julie's tear-streaked face so fresh in her mind. Julie, standing before an old ginger jar and a young boy's dog collection, weeping for that boy. Alice wanted to go home. Quickly.

'No,' she repeated, 'not today, Granny. Thank you.' She stood up, hoping she had not been too abrupt.

'You may read my glass of milk.' Julie quickly finished it and solemnly held the glass out to the old woman.

Alice laughed, grateful for this break in tension. 'Oh, Julie! Granny Goderich can't do that! Come and get your coat on. Don't move, Granny, I'll get them. They're on the bed, aren't they?' She left, glad to be released.

Granny Goderich took Julie's glass, its sides still opaque from the creamy milk. She shook her head sadly, looking into the eager little face.

'You're very young, Julie. You'll have to learn so much. People would think it strange if they knew we could tell things from a glass of milk or if they knew we didn't need glasses of milk or teacups at all. They can believe in teacups — teacups don't frighten them.' She cupped Julie's small solemn face in her hands. 'You'll learn.'

Alice bustled in with the coats.

'Perhaps you should let the car warm up a little, Alice. It's a bitter day.'

Alice wanted to be home. Now. Wanted to get Julie away. 'No, we'll be fine. Julie can hold her fur muff up if her nose gets cold. Can't you, dear? And the car warms up very quickly. We'll be fine.'

Julie sat huddled in the cold car, her head scrunched down in the soft fur collar of her coat. She did not hold her muff to her face at first — she puffed out clouds of white breath and watched them disappear. When, at last, she did press the muff to her reddening nose it held the musty odour of geraniums and she fell asleep.

CHAPTER FOUR

As Julie learned that she could no longer tell anyone her 'stories' she spent more and more time alone in the bush and fields of the Morgan farm. At first her mother was concerned. Alice Morgan was still haunted by those dark eyes that seemed to be seeing things she couldn't see.

'Where do you go, Julie? What do you do?'

Julie hadn't known how to answer until Charlie helped her. She was climbing through the fence behind the barn.

'Where you goin', kid? Exploring again?' he asked, lifting the strand of barbed wire above her so it wouldn't catch on her sweater.

'Exploring?' she asked.

'Oh, that's what you call it when you make an important trip to find out things, to learn about strange people or places.' Charlie couldn't help smiling at the eager look on Julie's face.

She had a smile that dazzled. Charlie realized that it might be because lately she smiled so seldom and the contrast to her sad, lonely look made the smile even brighter, like the sunburst after a storm. Now, as she beamed at him, he could almost feel the warmth.

'That's it!' her voice was exultant. 'I'm exploring. I'm exploring a tree I found in the sheep pasture.

Thank you, Charlie.' She turned and ran quickly between the strawstacks toward the pasture.

Charlie felt good. The kid could do that to you — make you feel as though you'd given her a million dollars when you'd only given her a word. He whistled as he walked toward the barn; it was his turn to clean it. He stopped whistling; he hated cleaning the barn.

Charlie had not only given Julie a word. He had solved the problem of explaining things to her mother.

'I'm going exploring,' she would say. And her mother would nod and smile and make motherly admonitions of where to go and which places to avoid. Then they would hug and Julie would go — her mother secure in the knowledge that Julie was all right and Julie proud of her discovery that if you called it 'exploring' it was all right to go looking for strange things and grownups would leave you alone.

Still, Julie was not five and although she was obedient, her mother worried if she was gone for too long. She got into the habit of sending one of the older children to check on her, 'Just to make sure she's all right, not hurt or anything.'

The report always came back the same. Julie would be sitting quietly under a tree watching insects, or birds, or just the movement of leaves and flowers. Once, when Joe found her, she was sitting very still staring at a cocoon that was spun around the twig of a rose bush.

'Nothing's happening there, Julie.' Joe poked at the dirty, white, matted-looking mass.

'Don't hurt it! It's getting ready to come out. It will be so happy. It's been shut up in there all winter. I don't want to miss it. Look . . . it's coming. Get your hand away from it.' Julie's voice, although urgent, was little more than a whisper.

Joe sat obediently beside her and stared for a minute. 'I don't see anything, Julie. You're full of baloney.'

'Shhh! There at that end,' she pointed, 'it's trying to break through.' Julie's eyes never left the twig. She seemed to be straining toward it.

Joe stared again. He could see no movement. Nothing at all.

'Aaaw, you're wasting your time. It's probably only an old cabbage butterfly, the kind Mum hates, anyway.'

'No, it's not. It's lovely. Big and brown with orange trim and even some little purple bits just above the eye marks on its wings. It's trying so hard, poor thing. That's it! Now!' Julie had spoken almost absently to Joe; her full concentration remained focussed on the cocoon which clung lengthwise along the stem.

Joe shook his head. There was no talking to this little sister of his. He looked at her staring at the twig, her face so still it seemed drained of life. Then a smile burst, dazzling him. It held him a moment before he looked back to the cocoon. The end Julie had pointed to was broken away and moving slowly out of it was a large fat something . . . like

36

a worm but fuzzy. Now the wings showed. Joe was amazed that such a large creature could have been inside that cocoon, and it was still growing. Right before their eyes the wings seemed to be expanding, trembling, growing.

'Wow,' Joe breathed, 'that's something!'

'Isn't it!' Julie caught his hand as he reached toward the moth. 'Be careful. It's got to dry off. It can't fly just yet.'

Joe let Julie pull his hand back. She was right. He didn't mean to hurt it but the deep richness of those velvet wings tempted him. She was right about the moth too. The brown, the orange, and those funny markings that looked like eyes now as the moth began to move its wings, slowly drying them. He let Julie hold his hand. A kid sister five years younger could get away with these things. Besides he was grateful to her for sharing this.

Later, when the moth had flown, they walked home together, not talking, the spell of the moth still on them.

At last, as they came through the fence of the sheep pasture — Joe over the top, Julie through the woven wire square headfirst like a rabbit — they could talk again.

'Julie, how'd you know it wasn't going to be a cabbage butterfly?'

Julie hesitated. ''Cause they come out of those hard brown things that look like a kind of sea-shell.'

Joe accepted this. If a person sat around all day staring at caterpillars and cocoons the way Julie did, you'd expect them to know a few unusual things a busy guy like him couldn't know. It was only natural.

He could see their mother standing at the kitchen door, dishtowel tucked in the top of her apron, waiting, and he realized they'd been a long time.

'Joe . . .,' she began, her voice sharp.

'It's okay, Mum. We were watching this moth come out of a cocoon and it took a while. Sorry.'

Alice Morgan relented. She had been worried but her annoyance had melted watching the two of them walking hand in hand across the field. It was good to see Julie so normal.

It happened that the one time Julie did get in trouble she did it in plain sight of the kitchen window.

Will Morgan had bought a big bay quarter-horse stud at a sale at Rocky Mountain House. Green broke, they said, but he soon realized it had never been ridden. He'd only had it a week.

The family were sitting around the table after supper when Mary screamed and pointed. They could see Julie climbing the corral fence beside the horse. She was small for her age . . . and beside that stallion she looked smaller than ever. He was right by the corral fence and when she got to the top rail, she grabbed his mane and slithered down his neck onto his back. There she sat, like an ant on an elephant.

Inside the house pandemonium broke out. Everybody raced for the door but their father got there first and turned them around.

'You'll spook him sure if you don't stay quiet.' His voice was calm, dead calm, but that didn't reassure them. Everybody who knew Will Morgan knew that the worse the situation, the steadier he became and his family knew this better than anyone. And they had never heard this flat tone of voice before.

He went out, closed the door quietly, and began to walk across the yard. Slowly.

Inside, they were all at the window again. Their mother fists pressed against her lips, moaning, 'Faster, Will . . . walk faster.' And Charlie, sounding more like his father than he knew. 'She'll be okay, Mum . . . Dad'll get her . . . It's okay, Mum.' The rest of them just held their breath and looked out that window.

It seemed to take years for their dad to get across the yard and all the time they could see Julie, her feet sticking out because her legs weren't even long enough to hang down the horse's sides. She kept petting the horse and talking to it and it never moved. Just stood there until Will got up to the fence and grabbed Julie off its back. Then the stallion snorted and wheeled away and raced around the corral. Nobody could get near it for a week, although Billy saw Julie sneak out with a carrot and pet its nose through the corral rails.

After that nobody objected to checking on Julie when she'd been away 'exploring' longer than usual.

Most of the time Julie was easy to find. There

was one particular balm of Gilead tree that stood apart from the other poplars at the edge of the pasture. It was the first place the other children looked when they were sent to check on her. Alice could see her if she was in front of the tree. But her favourite spot was at the back. A twisted root formed a seat where she could sit, her back against the trunk. She spent hours there.

Julie had talked to the tree almost from the beginning. She had always found trees friendly and liked to pat them as she walked along, but this tree seemed to be special. She would sit quietly. Talk or sing. The tree always welcomed her.

'Mum, do you know that Julie sits out there and babbles at that tree, on and on?' Mary reported once after a Julie-checking trip. 'Just nonsense. I can't even eavesdrop.'

Her mother nodded. She knew. She'd tried to eavesdrop once or twice herself. She wasn't sure it was nonsense — it sounded like words sometimes. Julie's voice rose and fell and there were inflections almost as if she was saying something.

'She sings too. More nonsense but at least there's a kind of tune.'

Her mother knew that as well. The first time Julie had seen the tree she had sung to it.

They were walking out to the field, taking lunch to Will so he wouldn't have to stop seeding. Julie was only three. Alice was enjoying the scent-soft spring air.

'Look, Julie,' she picked a leaf and put the sticky side on a scratch on Julie's arm, 'this is what I used

40

to use for bandaids when I was a little girl. It takes the sting away, doesn't it?'

Julie shut her eyes and held the leaf on her arm. 'Yes, it does. It feels all better.' She ran to the tree and looked up. 'Thank you, tree.' She began to circle around the big grooved trunk. 'Look, it's got a lap for me to sit in.' She sat down, leaned back, shut her eyes, and began to sing.

Her mother didn't recognize the song. It was chantlike but not at all the repetitive drone Julie used to sing herself to sleep when she was younger. There was a haunting lilt to this. The words were nonsense though. 'G . . . with, g'with, g . . . with g'with . . .' sang Julie, over and over.

'That tree is my special friend now, and I can visit it lots,' Julie had said as they went on.

CHAPTER FIVE

Although Julie spent most of her time alone by choice, she wanted company. She remembered Granny Goderich and the feeling she had when the old lady talked to her.

Sometimes when her mother announced, 'Dress up pretty today, Julie, we're going visiting,' Julie would rush around breathlessly finding good shoes and getting her coat and be standing waiting at the door long before it was time to go.

'Are we going to tea with Granny Goderich?' she'd ask when, at last, they were seated in the car.

The answer was always no, and it seemed to Julie that her mother was upset by the question so that finally she dressed quietly and went to the car never asking where they were going or if they'd see anyone she knew.

But she remembered.

Once in the spring she even tried to see Granny Goderich by herself. Joe said the school bus went by the Goderich's every day, so one morning Julie waited in the bush by the road until the others got on the bus and then ran after it. Joe said the bus moved 'like a snail. I can run faster!' But Julie couldn't. Couldn't even keep it in sight although she ran her fastest. Still, she went quite a way and she was still going, walking along in the ditch by the barbed wire fence to keep away from the dust the speeding cars threw at her, when her father drove up. He opened the door, rushed over to her, and caught her up, frightening a meadowlark from the long grass as he did so.

At first he didn't speak, just held her tight. Then asked, 'Julie, where are you going? You're more than a mile from home!' Julie felt sick. She couldn't tell him, didn't want to upset him as she had her mother but it was so hard to lie. She'd never lied to him, not even 'wiggled the truth so it fit' as Jane called it. She said nothing, just watched the meadowlark as it flew a few yards, then dropped one wing and began to flop across the ground. Will saw it too.

'Oh Julie, were you following meadowlarks looking for nests?'

Again Julie couldn't answer. She had never had to look for nests. She knew where they were. She had known ever since she could remember. Song sparrow nests tight in the branches of little spruce trees; killdeer nests that weren't really nests at all just hollows; the crowded nests of mallards and pintails in the long grass by the slough; nests like the one belonging to this flopping, floundering meadowlark. That nest was right beside the fence post less than a foot from the toe of Will's work boot. It had seven eggs.

Will smiled at her. 'Those birds are just trying to fool you. They'll keep flopping ahead of you, pretending to be hurt, making you think you can

43

catch them, until they've led you a long way from their nest and then they'll just fly away. No more wounded bird. They can fly just fine then.' Will moved toward the bird. 'See, Julie?' The bird fluttered away on cue.

Julie knew all about that. She'd watched Billy spend hours following 'wounded birds.' Billy never found nests and he looked so hard. Sometimes Julie would show him one of hers after he promised not to touch the eggs or the baby birds. She never showed any to the others. Joe and Jimmy took birds' eggs to school for the science corner.

He turned and strode through the ditch to the truck. 'You must promise me,' he said as he gave her a boost up to the high truck seat, 'that you'll never wander off like that again.'

Julie knew she hadn't been wandering. Even without the school bus she was sure she could find the Goderich place. She'd know when she got near it.

'Promise, Punkin,' he repeated.

'I promise I won't go away like that again,' said Julie carefully.

When they got to the corner by the sheep pasture, Will let her out so she could run home as he drove in the yard. Her mother had not noticed she was missing.

Julie didn't try to visit Granny Goderich again. She did not even think about her. Until she smelled the geraniums.

It was summertime and she was five. Her mother had never mentioned their visit again and Julie

44

talked less and less. She sat at the kitchen table after supper drawing a fly that was stuck on the toffee-coloured sticky paper spiral that hung in the kitchen window. Her mother wouldn't let her pull the flies off and let them go anymore so she drew them. Flying. Mary was helping their mother with the dishes. Everything was normal.

Then Julie smelled them. Geraniums. Musty, heavy geranium smell blocked her nose, pressed against her face, crushed her. For a moment she couldn't move. She knew there were no geraniums in the house. That year they had no geraniums anywhere. She dropped her pencil, leaving the fly eternally one winged, and ran out into the fresh evening air. But it wasn't. Not fresh at all. The summer evening that should have mixed a hundred smells and held the freshness of the breeze, pulsed with the smell of geranium.

Julie was afraid but she knew she had to do something. She couldn't stand the pressure building inside. The smell of a million geraniums.

Her father was in his workshop when she found him. She wanted to throw herself at him, cling to his greasy overall leg, and pull him to the truck but she held back.

'Daddy, if I asked you to do something very important, would you do it? For me? Now?' She rubbed her hand against her nose — hard — but the geraniums pressed in anyway.

'Sure, Punkin, I guess so.' He smiled at her, amused at her eagerness. 'You want me to make you something?'

'No. I want to go visiting. I have to see Granny Goderich.'

He smiled and ruffled her hair. 'I didn't know you and the old girl were such friends. Your mother didn't mention taking you there again. Come to think of it, she never mentioned what happened the time she did take you last winter.' He looked thoughtfully at Julie as if expecting an explanation.

Julie said nothing. It was so important that he understand or that he, like Julie, go without having to understand.

He smiled again, shaking his head. 'Why not? I don't mind doing a favour for a friend once in a while.'

Then Julie threw herself. Buried her face in his overalls that should have smelled of barn and machinery but only held the suffocating scent of geraniums.

Will held her hand as they walked to the truck, detouring past the kitchen door to call to Alice, 'Julie and I are going to return that welding torch to Behan's.' And privately to Julie on the way to the truck, 'Your mother would wonder and we'd have to explain things. We'll drop the torch off on the way back.'

Julie sat very close to him on the seat. The truck cab still held the day's heat and it churned with geraniums but the smell was almost bearable now.

The Goderich house was dark and still in the dusk half-light. 'Some of these old-timers never turn on a light until they have to. I remember when I was a boy my dad was always trying to save coal oil, now it's electricity.' His voice was easy but Julie noticed that he was walking faster than usual and she had to run to keep up.

There was no answer to the knock. He knocked again, louder. Behind him Julie felt the geraniums grow stronger. The odour circled her like a whirl-wind then pressed against her back so hard she nearly toppled. She slipped under his arm, opened the door, and darted in. Inside it was dark and writhing with the smell of geraniums but Julie did not stop.

Granny Goderich was lying in the parlour on the floor in front of the sideboard. The dark plants loomed and murmured against the window. She was very still but when Julie knelt beside her she caught Julie's hand and held it. Tight.

'Julie . . .', her voice was trembling, faint, 'I knew you'd come.'

Then her father was bending over them, lifting Granny onto the couch. 'Quickly, Julie, find the kitchen and get a glass of water.'

Julie didn't want to go, couldn't go until he pried her hand free of the old, blue-veined one that clung to hers.

'Julie . . .', the faint voice trailed after her to the kitchen. She could hear her father's voice.

'It's all right, Granny. What happened? Did you fall? When did it happen?'

Julie did not bother to turn on the kitchen light. Faster not to. She grabbed a glass, filled it, and was standing beside her father and Granny again.

Will had found the light switch and Julie could see now: the queue of dogs on the sideboard, the purple jar, the huddled geraniums everywhere — quiet now.

'Wednesday.' Granny's voice was just a whisper as Will held the glass to her lips.

It's Friday now, Friday night, Julie thought. She slipped her hand back inside Granny's and felt the old hand tighten, squeeze, and hold on.

'. . . forgot about Julie . . . couldn't move . . . couldn't call anyone . . . forgot about Julie.'

'Try to drink something, Granny. Julie, get a blanket. We've got to cover her, she's cold.' Will held Granny's head but some of the water dribbled on her chin.

'. . . not thirsty . . . could reach the watering can . . . forgot about Julie . . . all that time . . .'

'Julie, find a blanket.'

Julie couldn't move from Granny's side — the hand held her too tight. She reached up on the back of the puff-backed couch and pulled down an afghan with her free hand. It was bright and warm, made of pieces her mother called 'granny squares.' She realized that Granny's dress was wet and that a smell stronger than geraniums was making her eyes water.

'Where's the phone, Granny? I'll call Doc Barnes.'

'Julie . . . I forgot.' Granny's voice was far away.

'The phone's in the hall above the geraniums, Daddy,' Julie answered carefully, not looking at him. In a moment she could hear him dialling.

'You're a good girl, Julie . . . you came as soon as I remembered you . . . I forgot . . . memory's bad . . . too late . . .'

Julie touched Granny's cheek. Her skin was soft and tissue thin; it hung in tender folds on her neck. 'I didn't know what to do, Granny. I was afraid.'

'But you came, Julie. I should have called you sooner . . . all my fault . . . I forgot . . . You came . . .' Granny's hand gripped hers.

It's so strong, Julie thought. The other hand lay on the couch, limp and unmoving, like a dead thing.

'There's an ambulance coming to take you to Red Deer, Granny. Doc will see you in Emergency.' Will had found some old coats in the hall and he spread them over Granny. 'I called Mrs Behan — figured she could get here faster'n Alice — to get you some clean clothes . . .' his voice trailed off.

'She's resting,' said Julie. Granny's eyes were shut, her breathing soft.

'Maybe, if I can find a can of soup, I could heat some broth for her.' Will came and stood by Julie, his hand gently on her shoulder. 'You don't mind staying in here, Punkin? I shouldn't leave you alone, your mother —'

'I'm fine, Daddy,' Julie interrupted quickly. 'I don't mind and I think Granny wants me.' She did not look up.

Will ruffled her curls and left. Soon Julie could hear him opening and closing the cupboard doors. Granny opened her eyes.

'Don't be afraid. It's a gift. You did the right

thing.' Granny's voice was clear and firm. 'Times are different but you'll learn. You did the right thing.'

'I didn't know what it meant, Granny. I never know and so I don't know what to do.'

'That's how it is with us, Julie. We're not sure what to do . . . we're afraid. We don't know what to do and so we do nothing, nothing at all. Sometimes that's right, there's nothing we can do, sometimes . . .' Granny Goderich paused and Julie knew she was looking toward the old sideboard where the purple jar sat. When she spoke again it was with a sob.

'There comes a time when we have to act, like you did tonight. You have to decide and that's when the gift can be terrible. Wonderful and terrible . . ' The voice trailed off, tired. 'You have to learn when . . . you have to be strong. . . .' Slowly Granny closed her eyes.

Julie wanted to ask, How? How do I learn? But she couldn't now. She sat very still holding Granny Goderich's hand. She heard the door slam, voices in the hall, then her father and Mrs Behan bustling busy and Julie was shooed out, to wait in the truck and watch for the ambulance, they said.

It seemed to take a long time and then they were there, attendants rushing in with a stretcher and her father at the door of the truck, lifting her down.

'Granny wants you, Julie. She won't let them take her. She keeps asking for you. "Bring Julie," she says.'

Julie hurried into the house. Granny was still on the couch, wearing a clean nightgown, wrapped in a blanket. Her dead hand still lay unmoving but with the other, the strong one, she flailed at the two young men standing by the stretcher. 'Bring Julie . . . I want Julie.'

She was still as soon as she saw Julie, held her hand, and allowed Will and the men to put her on the stretcher and wrap her warmly. 'You'll be all right, Julie.'

Julie nodded, holding the hard-boned hand tight.

'I won't be coming back here,' Granny whispered, looking right into Julie's eyes. 'Do you understand, Julie?'

Julie nodded and let go.

As soon as the ambulance men, Will, and Mrs Behan had left the room with Granny quiet on the stretcher, Julie pushed a chair over to the sideboard and climbed up. She had to hurry but there were so many dishes and ornaments and she didn't want to break them or make a noise.

Close up, the jar was really a plum colour, not purple, and the swirls were parts of willow trees. Weeping willows. Julie picked it up carefully from among the dogs.

It was lighter than she'd thought it would be and the top was sealed on with a yellow, waxy stuff. She was relieved for it meant she could travel faster. She held the jar tight to her chest and climbed down. They were out in the yard now. She knew by the slam of the doors.

She ran out, glad to see that the men had stopped

to talk to Will and had not shut the ambulance doors. Mrs Behan was climbing into the front.

Julie slipped past the men and climbed into the back. She tucked the jar in beside Granny, felt her hand close on it, touched her cheek, and slipped back out before the ambulance men had turned around.

She was sure her father had seen her — he was facing the men and the back of the ambulance — but he didn't say anything until they were in the truck.

'What did you take to her, Julie?' His voice broke the comfortable motor-hum silence.

'Her Treasure, Daddy.' Julie knew he would understand that. Julie had a box of Treasures at home: a baby tooth the tooth fairy missed, a tiny tinkling bell Will had brought her from Calgary, a locket with some of her baby hair in it, a cracker-jack prize ring; and her piggy bank.

'Are you sleepy, Punkin?' was all he said.

Julie wriggled over, snuggled up to him, breathing the normal smells of father and truck; and fell asleep.

CHAPTER SIX

Will Morgan did not get to sleep so easily. Alice's questions did not stop even after they were in bed and the lights were out.

'How did you ever happen to be over by Granny Goderich's? That's not on the way to the Behan's.'

There were times when Will was grateful he was in the habit of speaking slowly — it gave him time.

'Oh, we were just driving a little. Such a nice night. I kinda thought I'd drive into Hurry and get Julie a treat. Maple buds.'

Maple buds were a joke in the family. Will always bought them for the kids. He was crazy about them.

Alice laughed, 'I might have known!' There was silence and then she spoke again, thoughtfully, 'How lucky that you did go by and notice the lights weren't on. Poor Granny Goderich. Do you know, I've never told anyone and I don't think anybody else knows, but she keeps little George's ashes in a ginger jar on the sideboard! She's mourned him all these years. A little purple jar on the sideboard. Imagine!'

Will remembered Julie slipping behind the ambulance, carrying something to Granny Goderich. It had looked like a jar but it was dark and she was cradling it. About the size of a ginger jar too.

'Good night, dear,' Alice's voice was soft, sleepy. She curled up in his arms as she always did to go to sleep. Before long he could hear her even sleep-breathing. He tried to relax and sleep himself, but he lay there long into the night. Wondering.

In the morning, he waited with Alice for Julie to come down to breakfast. Julie slipped into her chair, her face pensive as she slowly began to spoon up her porridge. He noticed that Julie's eyes were red as if she'd been crying, and he hoped Alice wouldn't notice and ask Julie any questions that might upset her more.

They were just sitting down beside Julie when the phone rang. Alice answered it and he could hear snatches, enough to know that it was Mary Behan phoning, then a long pause and Alice's voice changing tone, 'Oh, no!'

He looked over at Julie, who was staring very hard at a dead fly on the sticky paper. It was hard to read her expression. Drained, he thought, came closest. He could hear Alice softly replace the receiver and watched as she came in and sat down again, taking Julie's hand.

'Julie,' she said softly, 'Granny Goderich passed away early this morning.' There was no response and Alice tried again. 'Granny died in her sleep early this morning.'

Julie nodded. Her expression did not change. Her eyes were quiet, empty, Will thought.

'She was very old,' Alice said, 'and she'd had a stroke. That's why she couldn't move, you know.'

Julie nodded again, expressionless. She pushed her half-finished oatmeal away and got up from the table. 'Can I go out and play with the new kittens now?'

Alice nodded and watched Julie leave the kitchen before turning to Will. 'I know children are supposed to be matter-of-fact about death but Julie's always been so concerned about things dying. She's always rescuing flies or worrying about the baby plants when I thin the carrots. Remember the fuss she makes whenever the others pick wildflowers for me and forget to bring them in or put them in water?'

Will remembered. Remembered Julie, not much more than two years old, accosting Billy as he came in the yard, his grimy fist full of crocuses for his mother.

'They're dying!' she cried, her little face red and furious as she pushed him toward the water trough by the corral. 'You shouldn't have carried them so long. They're going to die!'

He knew Julie was the only one of the children who'd never brought Alice flowers. He'd never seen her pick a flower or pull a weed.

'Softhearted, the other kids call her. Especially after you had to sell that pony you bought her because she refused to ride him if he had to have a bit in his mouth.'

Will remembered that too. Julie refusing to ride Cocoa when Jimmy put a bridle on the pony, although she was a natural rider. 'Sticks like a burr bareback, Dad,' Jimmy'd announced after her first lesson. Jimmy's boast of making her 'Queen of the Rodeo' had fallen through abruptly when Julie cried at the gymkhanas because she decided that one of the ponies was unhappy or hurt. Everyone thought Julie hated riding but Will had seen her once out in the pasture, coaxing a horse over, scrambling up its leg and racing around the field. No saddle, no reins. Nothing. Just stretched out along its neck, her hair mixing with the mane. It was one of the things he had not bothered to tell Alice.

'I don't understand it, she's usually so concerned . . . so sensitive.' Alice shook her head sadly. 'Sensitive . . . that was Granny Goderich's word for her. I was afraid she meant something different.' Alice began to tidy the window ledge by the table. She picked up the papers Julie had been drawing on the night before. Flies. 'Look at the detail in these drawings. You think she'll grow up to be an artist or a scientist?'

Will was grateful when the phone rang and Alice went to answer it. He could tell that it was Mary Behan again, worrying about how to contact Granny's niece in Toronto. There were no relatives in the district. He could hear Alice volunteering to make some phone calls. Good. He hoped she wouldn't have time to worry about Julie's response to the news of Granny Goderich's death. He was even more grateful that she had not noticed that Julie's eyes were red this morning because he was afraid he knew why. Last night he carried her in from the truck and Alice slipped off her clothes and tucked her in bed. She had not been unhappy then, in fact she'd seemed somehow relieved. But sometime in the night, Julie must have awakened and cried. Sometime in the night, or early this morning. And Granny Goderich had died early this morning.

Granny Groderich's niece did not even bother to come out West. She arranged with the funeral director to have Granny cremated and sent to Toronto. Alice talked to Reverend Dickson and explained about the ginger jar that was being held with the neatly folded nightie and blanket at the hospital. Together they managed to convince the funeral director in Red Deer to mix the ashes and send them in one urn. Alice told Will she thought Granny would have liked it that way.

The Morgans were relieved that Julie did not seem to be scarred by the whole experience. She was not nearly as withdrawn as she'd been the week after the funeral. When Alice returned from her trip to Red Deer, Julie had been waiting to give her mother a hug and was the sunniest and most cheerful that Alice had seen her in a long time.

'It just shows,' Alice said to Will, 'it doesn't pay to brood on things. Everything generally works out and worrying about it never helps anyway.'

CHAPTER SEVEN

Julie went to the Goderich auction sale with her
father. Her mother was helping to run the Women's
Institute coffee and pie concession on the front
porch of the old house. It was not a big sale
and the local folks came mainly for the enter-
tainment. Any farm equipment worth having had
been sold when George Sr. died. What remained
in the machinery line was old horse-drawn equipment: ploughs, a mower, an old rake, some rusty
harrows with pieces missing. Granny Goderich had
managed to fill the house with a remarkable collection of things, though. Spread across the yard
it seemed hard to imagine them all fitting into
the six small rooms of the house. Some, like
the old pump organ with its pillared top and
mirrored brackets, were antique and valuable.
(Where had she kept it? folks wondered. Even
regular visitors couldn't remember having seen it.)
Others, like the bulky chrome kitchen set with its
shiny plastic seats spewing stuffing, were nearly
worthless. Still, there were quite a few strangers
in the crowd when the auction began: collectors
from Red Deer checking the old crockery butter
churn and the boxes of jars that had been stored
in the cellar; even a few antique dealers from
Edmonton drawn by the organ, the sideboard,

and Granny's ancient brass bed with its porcelain knobs.

The auctioneer began with some dishes and cracked vases now, and then selling a table or a plant stand, forlorn now without its geraniums.

From where she sat Julie could see everything. Her father had lifted her up onto the cab of the truck and she sat with her legs dangling down over the windshield being careful not to make scuff marks on her new black patent leather shoes. Theirs was the only vehicle parked in the yard except for the auctioneer's new car. The rest were crowded in the ditch and along the lane. Will had brought the coffee urns and the boxes of paper plates, cups, and other supplies. They'd come early and backed the truck right up to the porch. Now, he and some of the other men leaned against the front of the truck, but Julie could look right over their heads, over the heads of the crowd, right at the auctioneer.

She watched the people raising their hands to bid. Sometimes they nodded their heads when the auctioneer looked at them. Some of the ladies just flapped their sale lists at him.

Every time the auctioneer's helper bent to pick up one of the brown cardboard boxes Julie's excitement grew.

'One miscellaneous box!' he'd yell and start holding up some of the bigger things in it.

This time he picked up a white and blue enamel chamber pot.

'Now here's a handy all-purpose item!' Everyone laughed. 'You can use it as a spittoon, turn it upside down for a helmet in a hailstorm, or keep it under the bed in case the plumbing breaks down!' The crowd laughed again.

The auctioneer held up a few more things and then the bidding began.

Julie was surprised to see the box go for five dollars. The lady who got it rushed over and collected her box and brought it back to where her friends were standing near the truck. She dug through the sealers and loaf tins and then tossed out the auctioneer's 'spittoon' to lift out a butter dish with a glass cover and proudly show it to her friends.

'. . . drop and tassel . . .', Julie heard the lady say, '. . . not even a crack.' She looked very happy.

'I'll give you ten dollars for it,' said one of the other ladies but the lady with the butter dish just gave her a look.

They sold the old trunk from the hallway next. The top was all stained from the geraniums and when the auctioneer opened it up, it turned out to be full of old shoes.

Some people Julie didn't know bid on it; so did the ladies near Julie. It went for $18.50.

'Some people will buy anything,' one of the men beside Will said.

'City folks,' said another.

Julie watched for the miscellaneous boxes. Sometimes they went as high as $10.00. (That one had the pink china lady in it.) One of them, that just had sealers and a few cracked dishes, went for $2.50.

She could see the miscellaneous box she wanted. With two battered saucepans on top and some old cookie sheets under them you couldn't even see the dogs on the bottom. If only nobody had seen them. If only nobody wanted them.

She hugged her black plastic purse. It held $2.89 — all that had been in her glass piggy bank. Jane had showed her how to slide the coins out on a knife that morning. Piled on the quilt on her bed it had looked like a lot of money, now she wasn't so sure.

'One miscellaneous box,' yelled the auctioneer. 'Two saucepans, slightly used but still good for years.' He waved one in each hand. 'Ladies, if you can't cook, they're great for pitchin' at the old man!' He bent down, lifting out the cookie sheets, 'Cookie tins . . . some ornaments . . . dogs.' He held up the dalmatian with the broken leg. 'This one needs a vet! How much am I bid on this box of valuable items? Who'll start the bidding at five dollars?'

Julie's heart sank and she shut her eyes.

The auctioneer talked faster, 'Five, give me five . . . five dollars . . . Let's hear five dollars for this box of valuables.'

Julie opened her eyes. The auctioneer's bald head was shining in the sunlight and he was mopping at it with a red handkerchief.

'Tough crowd, eh? Okay, have it your way. Who'll give me one dollar to start?'

Several hands went up. Julie waved so hard she started to slip and had to flop back to catch herself. Will turned around.

'Watch the windshield, Julie.'

'One dollar! Who'll make it two? . . .'

Julie had her hand up waving again but the auctioneer was looking at a man wearing a brown suit jacket and blue jeans.

'One dollar and fifty cents . . . Do I hear two? Two dolla . . . dolla . . . dolla . . .'

This time he saw her.

'Two dollars from the little lady on the truck. That's called a high bid folks. Do I hear two-fifty?'

Julie could see the brown jacket man nodding his head.

'I have two-fifty, do I hear three? Just three dollars . . . three dollars and think of all the cooking you can do — porridge for the old folks, cookies for the kids — three dollars . . .'

Julie was just about to slide down the windshield to ask Will when she heard the auctioneer: 'I have three dollars . . . three-fifty? . . . Do I hear three-fifty? . . . Three-fifty . . . Do I hear four?'

Julie shut her eyes tight. She'd lost them. All the funny little dogs Granny had saved all these years. George's dogs.

'Going once! Going twice! Sold for three-fifty! . . . Planning on doing some cooking, eh Will?'

Julie's eyes snapped open. Her father was walking toward the truck, the miscellaneous box in his arms. As he passed the men, Paddy Behan nudged the man next to him. 'Some folks buy anything!' They all laughed.

'Thank you, Daddy,' Julie whispered as she

The leaves' song seemed quicker and brighter. 'Charlie says I'd better learn to read quick 'cause I'm drivin' him crazy always asking him to read about the pictures in the old *Books of Knowledge* that Mum has.'

Julie put her arms as far as she could around the trunk, her face pressed against the wrinkled bark. It was silky and yielding. She felt if she pressed very hard she could move inside and become part of the tree. Fold up inside it like a leaf inside a bud in the spring. The warmth and softness seemed to flow through her, smoothing out the rumples of worry. Had she been afraid? She couldn't seem to remember why. She knew how to be quiet. She would be very careful. It was, after all, just the first day of school.

'I'll hurry out and tell you all about it as soon as I get home. I can look forward to that,' she whispered.

She stood there a long time, until the bark felt hard against her cheek and she could hear her mother calling her for supper.

School really wasn't so bad. She kept quiet and tried to listen and not think of something else even during arithmetic. She was the first one in grade one to begin reading that year.

Reading was great. You could hide in a book nearly as well as in the bush. The stories were almost better than seeing things because you could talk about them without anyone getting upset or calling you a liar. All you had to do to prove you weren't was to find the page and point to it.

Books soon replaced the stories her Granny Morgan had come in the night to tell her when she was little and by the end of the year she could read the stories about Merlin and Camelot herself.

She had an ally at school in the unlikely person of Miss Johnson, the librarian.

Billy could not believe it when Julie told him she thought Miss Johnson was the nicest teacher. 'Johnson! You're kidding! It was a great day for the kids when the school board decided to stick her in the library. I had her for half of grade two and she never got off my back the whole time. Never let me forget that she taught Dad and "there never was a harder working boy than Will Morgan". There was dancing in the halls when Johnson retired to the library!'

Julie didn't argue. It was actually a secret friendship anyway. It had started one day after a library class in which Julie's teacher had made her put back the books she'd selected.

'I don't think T. H. White's *Sword and the Stone* is suitable for a grade two student. Why don't you take the Walt Disney version?'

Julie looked at the book the teacher was handing her. It was mostly pictures and hardly any story at all. 'But I can read the words — ', she began.

'Grade Twos take books from the shelf marked Grade Two.'

Julie took the book of course but later, when she was going to the bathroom, Miss Johnson called her into the library.

'Juliet, if you finish your books before the week is up, come to the library after school and you may have some others.'

It seemed to Julie to be a wonderful present and she tried to thank Miss Johnson but that lady ignored her thanks and fell to stamping the returned books with unnecessary vigour.

Gradually Julie had changed. She hadn't even noticed it happen. Just that she didn't let herself think about anything unusual anymore — not after she learned about Joan of Arc.

There was a picture in the *Book of Knowledge* Julie had been drawn to long before she started school. A picture of a beautiful, young girl in armour tied to a post with logs piled up around her and a fire at her feet. It seemed to Julie that she had always looked at that picture. Finally someone told her the story of Joan of Arc. She cried the first time she heard it but it was still the first picture she turned to whenever she looked in that book. As soon as she could read well enough she read the story for herself. It was then she found out about Joan's voices.

She had been buoyantly happy when she'd learned about the voices. She wasn't the only one — that beautiful girl had been different too. Not normal.

The happy feeling hadn't lasted long. She'd soon learned it was the voices that got Joan into all that trouble.

It was then Julie began to be careful not to touch the wedding gown quilt patch when she went to bed at night. She made sure that she had a book to read and fall asleep with.

Sometimes she remembered the stories she had heard in the night when she was younger, especially when she read one about the ancient women who had become tree spirits. But it was safer to read stories. Safer not to hear things other people couldn't hear.

CHAPTER NINE

For over a year nothing strange happened. Then it wasn't voices Julie worried about, but a smell. A smell that shouldn't have been there. Like the geraniums.

Julie had wakened that morning feeling uneasy. The smell was so strong. What was it? She'd smelled something like it before. Then she remembered.

It was mouse smell. The bedroom smelled just like the old Tyler house, empty all the years Julie could remember. Even Charlie said that it had always been empty. For a while the Morgans had stored grain in the big front room but the floor was caving in now and the house was not used. The children were not supposed to go there but they did, of course. Even Julie.

They were careful of gaping holes in the floor and the rotting stair steps. It was a good place to explore, to rummage in the bedrooms in the old newspapers and magazines. There were still old bottles and broken dishes in the pantry. Once Julie had found a doll's teapot that only had the handle missing.

The last time she'd gone with Jane and Billy, Jane had come in, stood in the old kitchen, and sniffed. 'Mouse. This house is full of mice. I'll wait for you outside.'

Julie had noticed the smell that day — strong in the stuffy rooms in the heat of the summer sun.

It was the same smell in the bedroom this morning. It seemed to fill the room, a strong horrid smell, and she knew there were no mice here. Julie began to tremble. There were no mice, but there had been no geraniums either.

In the pale early-morning light she could see Jane in the other bed. She looked very still and was breathing loudly.

Last night Jane hadn't been still. She'd been crying and tossing in her sleep. Julie remembered being wakened by it and by Alice coming in and sitting beside Jane's bed talking to her softly. Once, Julie had got up and tried to give Jane a drink but Jane swung her arm and knocked the glass out of Julie's hand. It was frightening. Jane didn't seem to know her, moaning and thrashing about in the bed. That time, when Alice came Jane had finally been quieter and Julie had gone back to sleep.

The mouse smell was so strong. It had never bothered her in the Tyler house but now it gave her a choking feeling. She thought of Granny Goderich. Jane was so pale.

Julie climbed out of bed wriggling her toes in the sheepskin mat by her bed before she set out across the cold linoleum floor.

She looked up to see her mother standing in the doorway.

'What's wrong, Julie?' There was a pause as Alice Morgan took a deep breath. 'Do you smell something?'

Her mother's voice was worried, urgent. Why was she asking that? Julie knew her mother watched her a lot. She'd done that ever since Julie could remember. Worrying about Julie seeing things. Now it would be Julie smelling things. Mice when there were none.

Julie would not be caught. 'Jane's awfully sick,' she said. Standing closer to Jane's bed she could smell the mice even more. She tried to remember if the geranium smell had changed.

Her mother moved across to Jane's bed. Her hand reached out to Jane's forehead automatically.

'Don't you smell anything, Julie?' she asked again.

Julie climbed back into her own bed and sat knees to chin under the blanket. Did she have to answer? Maybe if she didn't her mother would forget to ask again.

'Will,' her mother called.

The look on her face frightened Julie but not as much as the mouse odour that clung to her nostrils.

Her father appeared in the doorway. Julie was not much comforted by his presence. Even with his help Granny Goderich had died.

'She's worse?' he said. 'I could probably catch Doc Barnes before he leaves for the hospital . . . might be time to — Good Lord, where'd the mice come from?' He sniffed audibly.

Julie sat very still hugging her knees, not breathing.

Her mother's voice was strange; muffled, not like the sure, clear tone Julie knew. 'Mother said they smelled mice the time her little sister died of diphtheria . . .' Her voice rose. 'Will?' It was not really a question, more a cry.

'I'll phone Doc.' He was already down the hall and Julie could hear the back ring as he dialled.

They could smell it! Both of them smelled it. Julie was out of bed standing across Jane's bed from her mother.

'You smell it, don't you Julie? Like mice?' Alice did not turn her worried face from Jane so she did not see the relief, almost joy, on Julie's face.

'Yes, Mum. Oh yes! I smell it!' The mouse smell wasn't like the geraniums after all, it was real. Maybe it was not normal, but it was not something only Julie knew about. 'Jane'll be all right, Mum, you'll see!'

There was such confidence even exuberance in Julie's voice that her mother managed a weak smile.

'Run along and call Mary to start breakfast. You shouldn't be in here.'

'I had my shots for that diphtheria stuff, Mum,' Julie said, heading for the door, 'we all did. Except Jane.'

Her mother's voice was sharp. 'What? Jane didn't? Why ever not?'

'She was away sick one time and one time she hid in the washroom. She hates needles. I think she had one shot because she was real mad that Mrs Heppler, the health nurse, wouldn't believe

74

she didn't get the other shots. I think the cards got marked wrong.'

'Jane sneaked her card out and marked it herself while Heppler was having coffee with the teachers.' Joe was standing in the doorway. 'We told her it was a dumb thing to do but we couldn't very well snitch on her, Mum, could we?' Joe's voice trailed off as he recognized the look on his mother's face.

Her mother shook her head, her face very tired. 'Go help get breakfast both of you.' She waved a distracted hand at them, her eyes still on Jane's face.

Her father was still sitting at the phone, shoulders hunched, when Julie went by. She paused, slipped her hand into his, and looked at him.

'She'll be okay, Daddy,' she said softly.

He held her hand to his cheek and looked at her in the steady way he had, right in the eyes, for a long time. 'You've got your Great-Granny Morgan's eyes, Julie,' he said at last. 'I wish you could have known each other.' He gave her a quick hug and was walking down the hall to the bedroom. She heard him say, 'Doc Barnes will be out as soon as he can,' as he shut the door.

Breakfast was not the usual noisy affair. Even when Billy knocked over his milk, the others forgot to remind him that it was the third, or sixth, or fourteenth time he'd done it that week the way they usually did.

Joe suggested that since nobody was paying attention to them they might as well miss the school bus but Mary and Charlie herded them out just as Dr Barnes's car pulled into the yard.

Julie had been right. When they got home from school Jane was already improving. There was the usual concern over someone sick but her mother's worried look was gone.

The mouse smell had not been a sign like the geraniums; everyone could smell it. But that was last year when she was nine, when she'd just begun to think she was going to be normal. Instead, after such a long time, it had happened again. Not voices, or smells, but ships. Old-time ships sailing across a field in the middle of Alberta. There wasn't a chance that anybody but Julie would see that, and she knew it.

Julie walked across the field, feeling the black, freshly ploughed clumps of earth break under her feet.

Across from her, on the hill, stood the house. An ordinary farmhouse. Her mother and Mary were out trying to untangle the sheets now. Jimmy was in front of the barn grooming his pinto. ('It's a wonder that animal's skin isn't worn out,' Charlie said.) Jane was coming out of the chicken yard with a pail. Eggs probably. Normal: boy and horse, mother and daughters, even the house with the red geraniums.

Jane had been allowed to choose the flowers for the window box this year. They took turns. Julie would never have picked geraniums; they reminded her too much of Granny Goderich. She wished Jane hadn't but then Jane didn't know. Nobody knew. Julie couldn't tell anyone that either.

At least she had somehow known what to do about the geraniums, there had been such urgency. The ships were different. Not impelling her to act but . . . what? Telling her something she was sure, but she was just as sure that she wasn't getting the message. All she knew was that she couldn't tell anyone nor could she shake off the uneasy feeling they gave her.

Julie reached the edge of the field and sat down on a big rock by the corner post to empty the dirt out of her shoes. She climbed up on the rock, put her foot on the rail that angled up to the other corner post like a prop, balanced a moment, and then jumped down on the other side, almost falling, catching herself with her hands so she didn't. Granny Goderich might have known how to explain the ships. It would be different if Granny Goderich were here. A friend, someone to talk to. But Julie was alone. Except, of course, for the tree.

She was headed there now, automatically, without thinking about it or deciding that it was where she should go.

She ran the last bit of the way and sat down in her place. She felt she'd been holding back as long as she could bear but she waited, her cheek against the rough bark, listening to the tree.

The heavy dark leaves above her started suddenly, as if from somewhere a small whirlwind had passed through. Then it was very still and she opened her eyes, staring at the uneven bark, its smooth ridges and rough grooves against her face. She felt the creased bark soften. It comforted her as it always did and she relaxed a little.

Only a little. For when she closed her eyes she saw them again. The ships. Just as she had seen them. Floating on the black field in the hot sun. Silent as ghosts.

'Why?' It was really a cry not a question. She knew now that there was no hope of an answer in the murmuring leaves. 'It's been such a long time. I thought I was over it and now it's come back and it's worse than ever.'

There was a breathlessness, even in the shade of the tree, that Julie thought was not altogether because of the heat of the afternoon. It seemed to weigh her down. She wondered how the leaves managed to continue their murmuring when the day was so still, so heavy. She slept.

When she arrived home, hot and tired again, Billy was moving across the yard with his arms full of wood.

CHAPTER TEN

'We're having a wiener roast for supper. Mum and Dad are going to be home late. Hurry up. Mary says you'd better get in there and help carry things out.'

Julie headed into the kitchen and stood quietly inside the door.

'Look who's here at last! Now that all the work's done!' Jane, under the weight of a jug of lemonade, bustled by giving Julie an unnecessary bump as she did. 'Outta my way. Why aren't you ever around when you're needed?'

Julie said nothing, waiting for Mary to give her orders.

'You forgot the time again, I suppose.' It wasn't a question. Mary didn't even sound upset, just matter-of-fact. The family had long ago given up on Julie as far as keeping track of time was concerned.

'Julie doesn't march to a different drummer,' their father told them, 'she doesn't have a drummer beating time for her at all.' She had tried to pay attention to the time and her mother gave her a wrist watch every year for Christmas but the watches just ran slower and slower and finally stopped and couldn't be fixed. When Mrs Morgan sent them back because the guarantee wasn't up, the watch company just sent her a new watch and the same thing would happen again. Finally her mother gave up. Her father said time was not Julie's problem, it was everybody else's.

'I'm sorry,' Julie said. And she was. She always was. She held her arms out for the bowl of potato salad Mary handed her. It was cool from the fridge and she held it tight against her savouring the pleasant shock of cold.

'Tell Billy, just a little fire. It's so hot, I hate the thought of a fire at all, but you kids will have to have your wiener roast, I guess.'

Julie moved out slowly, carefully, cradling the salad, pushing backwards against the screen door until she felt it pulled open and looked up to see Charlie holding the door. His face was streaked with sweat but he was smiling down at her. 'Don't drop that, kid. D'you want me to carry it for you?'

She shook her head, smiled back, and walked carefully out into the heat of the yard. Even now, at five o'clock, it hadn't let up. The heat rose in waves from beneath her feet, buffeted her head. Under the trees it was only a little better; so still she felt that she would smother. She set the bowl on the picnic table and waited, hoping for some small breeze, a stir of air, just a puff of wind so that she could breathe. Nothing. She took a big gulp of hot air, 'Mary says, just a little fire, it's too hot.'

Billy didn't seem to notice the heat. He was arranging the wood very carefully, like a tall teepee, placing one stick on top of another patiently, as though he were building a card house. Julie walked slowly back across the yard.

Even without any cooking going on, the house was hot. It seemed to be hotter with cupboard doors slamming open and shut. Jane opened a drawer and glared at it. Mary, wisps of hair escaping from her ponytail and pasted against her cheek, was on the floor, half into the cupboard, removing everything with grim determination. Behind her sealers of all sizes ranged in disorderly battalions.

'Julie,' her voice showed even Mary's patience was about to give, 'do you know where Mum keeps the paper plates? We've looked everywhere.'

Julie stepped carefully around the sealers, got the kitchen stool, moved it over in front of the fridge, and climbed up. She opened the door of the small cupboard above, where her mother kept the good glasses, and took out a package of paper plates. Without saying anything she climbed down and carried them outside.

The kitchen was silent except for fly drone, then Mary began putting bottles back into the cupboard.

'How does she do it?' Jane demanded of the drawer, 'She always manages to find things.'

Mary sighed, 'I should have asked her in the first place.'

The sky darkened early and it cooled off a little. Replete, the seven young Morgans sat around the fire. Joe and Jimmy were making up 'crossing' riddles.

81

'If you cross an automatic transmission with your backside, what do you get?'

Julie did not play. She sat on the end of one of the log benches and stared into the fire. She didn't care for bonfires — they made her think of Joan. Sometimes she could see Joan, her face no longer serene, her head twisted against the cross the soldier had made her that was just two pieces of wood bound together with a cord. Then flames and smoke would blot her out and when it cleared again she would be crumpled down against the ropes and the cross would be burning too. Julie got up and turned away from the fire.

'A shiftless bum!' yelled Joe. The others groaned and threw grass and small sticks in appreciation.

'Julie,' Mary called, 'if you're going to the house bring back that package of marshmallows on the counter.'

Relieved to be doing something, Julie headed toward the still, dark house. She stood for a long time in the kitchen, the close darkness pressing against her as though she were enveloped by the wings of some huge bird. Then, fumbling along the counter until she found the soft package, she left without turning on the light and stood for a moment on the porch. There was a breeze now and it lifted the dark tendrils of hair that curled tight against her forehead. She could breathe again. By the fire, her brothers and sisters laughed and shouted and she watched them, envying their easy play. She started to walk slowly back to the fire.

As she turned to look back toward the house she

saw flames coming from the top of the hill behind it. The granaries were burning! Orange tongues licked up the walls and along the shingles, biting into the sky and the black night hillside. The granaries were on fire and nobody had noticed.

Julie turned and started to run. 'Char—' she began calling and stopped. Standing still, she clamped her eyes tightly shut and very slowly turned to face the hill. She opened her eyes gradually hardly daring to breathe.

The hill was dark and still. She stared into the darkness. If she had not known the granaries were there she would not even have noticed the two black shapes. She turned toward the campfire and back to face the hill again. She concentrated on breathing evenly — in, out ... in, out — as she walked steadily toward the others.

'We have to let the fire die down, the wind's comin' up. You kids can do your marshmallows over the coals but hurry, we'll have to douse this good before we go in.' Charlie sounded just like his father. 'There's gonna be a storm. I hope the folks get home first.'

Julie lingered outside after helping Mary and Jane carry the dishes into the house. She watched Joe and Jimmy carry pails of water to the fire. The wind was stronger now, scooping feathers up in the chicken yard and chasing them into the darkness beyond the fire. A plastic pail on the step flipped and bounced across the yard. She stayed out until all the others had gone in and Charlie stood, holding the door, waiting for her. There was a distant rumble of thunder and some faint sheet lightning on the horizon. The hill was wrapped in darkness. She ran gratefully toward the house and the open door.

Later, lying in bed upstairs across from Jane, Julie waited for the lightning flashes that would wash their room with light. She listened to Jane counting the seconds before the thunderclaps.

'Five miles away! They're coming closer!'

Jane's excitement did not touch Julie. She only squirmed deeper under her old quilt so that the flashes could not intrude through her closed lids.

The crashes grew louder. Nearer if Jane's counting meant anything. Julie listened. Once or twice Jane could hardly squeeze a number in, then the pause became longer. Jane was asleep before the first over-ripe drops of rain began to pummel the shingles above them. Julie lay awake a long time thinking.

She wakened to a strange feeling. Thoughts shifted across her mind like a kaleidoscope, changing restlessly. Sun streamed in, dust dancing in the beams. She went to the bathroom to wash.

Voices drifted up the stairs. Her mother was talking to Mary.

'Don't know when it happened. . . . There were some pretty loud thunderclaps just after we got home, though. It's a good thing they didn't have much grain in them . . . should have lightning rods, I suppose.'

The shifting, restless feeling slowed. Julie finished dressing and started slowly downstairs.

The window on the landing faced the hill. She looked out not noticing the fresh, rain-washed morning, seeing only the hill where her father and Charlie moved about kicking charred bits of board and the blackened remains of grain, all that was left of the granaries.

She watched them quietly. She had seen the fire and she had done nothing. The turning thoughts settled into place. You can't stop lightning. It happens. Julie remembered Granny Goderich. Sometimes it's all right to do nothing. There's nothing we *can* do. She felt very calm . . . strong.

She walked the rest of the way down the stairs and into the kitchen. The voices of her mother and Mary rushed toward her, excited, telling her what had happened.

Julie felt very good. She had done the right thing by keeping quiet.

CHAPTER ELEVEN

Julie sat on the bottom step, her bare feet warm on the smooth stone in front of the kitchen door. A wasp buzzed around her knees but she didn't move. She was eavesdropping.

'. . . the worst part, Will, is that I can't afford to go and I can't afford not to.'

'Now, Alice, she's your last relative on your mother's side; she practically raised you after your mother died. We'll just have to find the money. If she needs you, you should go.'

Julie knew who they were talking about. Great Aunt Emma. She used to come and visit them while Julie was little before Aunt Em got sick and couldn't travel any more. 'Aunt Em should be like a grandma to you, Julie, she was like a mother to me,' Alice had said. She was not the kind of grandma Julie imagined. She was very thin and straight and smelled of mothballs. She had a nice smile, though. The Granger smile, people called it. They said Julie had inherited it.

The voices in the kitchen were rising; her mother's was becoming strident.

'. . . so we find the money, borrow it or something, and I go and she isn't as bad as they think and next month she really needs me but I don't know if I should go . . . it's so awful . . . I never even know whether to be relieved or not when they turn out to be wrong. Just lying there in the nursing home, existing, is all she's done. When she has what they call a "good day" it just means that she's not in pain for a change. Why didn't I bring her to a home in Red Deer when she took sick and couldn't stay alone any more?'

Her father's voice softened to a sigh, 'We've been over that. She wanted to stay in Victoria. She thought she'd be getting out again and you're so softhearted you went along with it, putting her furniture and things in storage, helping her to look forward to an apartment. Besides, she had friends to visit her there.'

Julie heard her mother's voice. It was a remembering voice now. 'She hated the prairies, but I never knew it. All those years hating the winters, the frost on the walls of that old farmhouse, the summers that shrivelled her garden and stunted those roses she was always trying to grow ... hated it and never said anything until after Grandpa died. Kept house for him on the farm all those years, raised me, and never said a word. Then Grandpa died and I was through school, working in town, and she sold the place and was off to the coast before I realized what was happening. All she wanted was a place where she could grow roses all year round. She'd hated it all those years and I never even noticed ... never saw ... she was just Aunt Em ... always the same, always there.'

'So you be there. Be there when she needs you. We'll find the money.'

'I know you will, dear, I know. But still, it's a shame to keep running back and forth. Plane fare to Victoria isn't that cheap. If only I knew when I should go . . . I just hate the thought of not being with her when it's time but I can't just go dashing back and forth even if you do manage to find the money!'

Julie moved silently around the house and crouched under the kitchen window, waiting.

'It's money you need for other things, Will . . .' the voice trailed off.

Julie heard the screen door slap shut. Her father, she knew, was walking toward the woodpile. She could not see him but she knew how he would be walking, head down and determined. He would chop wood steadily, axe rising and falling, blocks halved neatly and cleanly with one stroke. The pile of split wood was a gauge the family used to know how upset their father was over something.

Julie waited, listening for the sound of the axe.

In the kitchen, her mother would be sitting at the oilcloth-covered table, her head in her hands. Julie knew that too. She did not have to bother standing up and looking through the flowers in the window box into the kitchen.

She knew so many things without looking, naturally, without knowing how she knew. But what good was it?

It was going to be another hot day and the odour of the geraniums in the window box drifted down to her, clogging her nostrils the way it had at Granny Goderich's long ago when she was little. Granny Goderich would have told her what to do.

And then Julie knew.

She stood up, her head narrowly missing the heavy wooden window box. She stood very straight for a moment and then walked around to the kitchen door.

Her mother was indeed sitting at the table, head in hands. She did not look up.

Julie went to the stove and put on the kettle. She climbed up on a chair and reached down the old tea canister.

'What *are* you doing, Julie?' Her mother's voice was tired but patient.

'I'm making you a cup of tea. You look tired and you always say "a cup of tea never hurts and it might help" to Daddy.'

Alice Morgan smiled sadly. 'That's what Aunt Em always used to say to me.'

Julie hugged herself tightly as she waited for the kettle. When the water was boiling she poured some into the teapot, swished it around, and emptied it into the sink. Then she carefully spooned the tea into the pot and poured again. She took down a good china cup and saucer and carried it and the teapot to the table.

Her mother smiled. 'You remembered to "hot the pot" did you, Julie?'

Julie nodded. 'Like you showed me.'

'Like Aunt Em showed me,' her mother said softly. She lifted the lid and glanced inside.

'Julie, why didn't you use a teabag? This stuff is as old as the hills.'

'It needs leaves, Mummy. I'm going to read your teacup.'

Julie could see her mother's body tighten, the teacup paused halfway to her lips. She felt the look and raised her eyes to meet it.

For what seemed ages their eyes held each other. 'Like Granny Goderich, Mum,' Julie said, pleading.

At last her mother looked down at the tea. 'Thank you, Julie,' she said softly, raised the cup, and drank.

Julie felt a little breathless. She rubbed her palms hard on her cotton shorts to dry them. She watched as her mother turned the empty cup upside down in the saucer and handed it to her.

Julie shut her eyes. Now she had to know. Had to be sure. She opened them. She was staring at the calendar on the wall behind her mother. It was from Norton's Garage in Hurry. They gave out two calendar pictures. Julie had been with her father when he got this one. He had left the one of the blonde lady in the cowboy hat peeking over her shoulder, her guns and holster longer than the black satin shorts she wore, and had picked the one of a little girl holding a puppy. A little girl with a small heart-shaped face and a tangle of dark curls.

'She looks like you did when you were three,' he said.

Julie stared at the little calendar girl's eyes. Large brown eyes that looked directly at you and followed you around the kitchen. She had to be sure. She looked at the numbers beneath. They were red with the numbers of holidays hollowed out. Then the number ten turned black and began to grow away from the paper toward her.

She took a deep breath and she could smell them the way she had smelled the geraniums long ago. Mothballs. She glanced at the teacup.

'You will,' she said in a voice she hardly recognized as her own, 'receive bad news on the tenth.' Suddenly Julie felt very cold. Almost shivering in the warm kitchen. 'That's all,' she said in her own voice, not looking up from the cup.

'Thank you.' Her mother's voice was loud and unnatural too. She stood up and moved into the hall. Julie heard her lift the telephone receiver and begin dialling.

Through the kitchen window Julie could see her father chopping steadily, sweat staining an oval on his shirt between his shoulders. Had she done that right? Shouldn't there have been things about dark, handsome strangers and getting letters and taking trips?

She stared at the soggy jumble of tea leaves in the bottom of the cup, then crossed the kitchen and scooped them out into the garbage. She could hear her mother's voice asking about the flight times to Victoria.

CHAPTER TWELVE

Alice Morgan appreciated the drive home from the airport in Red Deer; it gave her a chance to relax and tell Will about her trip to Victoria and her brief time with Aunt Em before the frail woman had lapsed into unconsciousness.

'You know, Will, I never realized how little we said to each other. Oh, we talked all right but all those years we said things like, "Are you cold?" and "Are you hungry?" I never realized until she said, "Are you happy, Alice?" that we had never let on how we felt. She hated the farm all those years, you know, and she never said a word. I never knew until she moved away.'

She told him of the night-time vigil by the bed-side, half-asleep herself sometimes, and of the end.

'At least I got there in time. She was still able to talk and not in any pain, just very weak. And I think she knew I was with her even during the hours she was unconscious. I'm so glad I went when I did.'

'When you phoned you said she died early in the morning.'

Alice nodded. 'The morning of September 10,' she said softly. She had not told Will the reason for her sudden decision to go to see her aunt or why she had gone when she did.

They made the familiar turn and could see down the road to the farm. The yard. Home.

'Oh look, Will, there's poor Billy getting another riding lesson and poor Jimmy giving it.'

They could tell when Billy saw the car; he called out and slid off the horse. Then the rest of them running out of the house: Joe and Jane, Charlie and Mary.

'Looks like I'm not the only one who missed you, Alice. Quite a welcoming committee.'

'Oops, Mary's forgotten the dishtowel. Hiding it behind her back, that'll fool me! I'll never guess they've been in there frantically cleaning house ever since you left home this morning. Fatheads, I do love them all. Where's Julie?'

'There she is coming from the barn.' He stopped the car. 'Who's in charge here?' he yelled as they climbed out. 'There's luggage to be carried in.' But they were too busy to pay attention and he carried it himself.

Through the jumble of hugs and greetings Alice could see Julie, waiting her turn. I don't think I can face those eyes. I don't want to talk about it, but she's puzzled, waiting for me to make the first move. What do I do? Julie was right . . . she knew. Without even knowing how to read a teacup or any of the formula stuff, she knew. And she's waiting.

Now it was Julie's arms around her. 'Welcome home, Mummy.'

'Thank you, darling.' Then softly in Julie's ear, 'I'm so glad I went when I did. I got there just in time.' She felt Julie stiffen slightly. That's enough.

Leave it, she thought, neither of us wants to talk about it.

'I missed you, all of you, so much. Come in the house and help me unpack. I've got a little present for you, for each of you.'

Julie stood waiting, one leg wrapped around the other, looking awkward but really comfortable, while her mother unpacked.

'Julie first!' Alice began to unwrap something that was bundled in a pink towel. A dog. A large liver-coloured setter, nose pointing, foot raised forever.

'There! It's for your collection, Julie. It was Aunt Em's. Isn't it beautiful?'

'Oh no,' wailed Jane. 'She's already got her crummy dogs all over our dresser. I can see it. There'll be no room for any of my stuff. I'll barely have a corner. I'll have to get a smaller comb. I'll —'

The others laughed her down.

'Never mind, Julie,' Charlie was saying. 'I'll build you one of those little knick-knack shelves you can hang on the wall. Then Lady Jane can have the whole dresser for her giant comb.'

'. . . for her giant head!' added Joe, ducking behind Jimmy.

'You won't put the shelf too high, Charlie. I want to be able to reach them.'

'No, kid, you'll be able to take your dogs down and play with them whenever you want.'

'Just don't let them get on the dresser and poop on Jane's comb!' hooted Billy and fled.

Julie watched him take off with Jane in hot pursuit. There was no point in telling Charlie that she didn't play with the dogs. It was so nice of him to make the shelf, such a good idea. She watched her mother, laughing, telling them to 'settle down and look at what else there was'.

Her mother caught Julie's eyes and smiled. Julie beamed back. No more teacups. Everything was lovely and normal. Granny Goderich had been right. If you used a teacup, it was all right. Nobody thought anything of it.

She wondered, as she climbed into bed that night, if she would someday be able to handle things like the ships as easily. Next library period she would sign out the ship book she'd seen on the reference shelf. There might be something there that would help her understand.

CHAPTER THIRTEEN

'Juliet,' Miss Lundgren's voice was sharper than she intended it to be. 'What are you doing with that picture book? Get a book to read!'

Miss Lundgren was having difficulty maintaining the necessary severity. Mr Kendal, the principal, had particularly told the new teachers to be very strict for the first two weeks because 'it kept the kids in line the rest of the year.' But it was hard for her. 'Let them know how soft you are and they'll walk all over you,' her friend Sonia had warned her. The trouble was, it was as if the class was perfectly familiar with Mr Kendal's dictum. There was an air of patient expectancy about them, as if they were waiting for September to be over so they could find out what she was really like.

It was awkward, too, trying to get to know the class while still maintaining her own artificial air. This Julie Morgan, for instance, sitting there poring over the forbidden picture book, *Brigs, Barkentines, Schooners, and Ships*, seemed to be such a forlorn, dull little creature. Never, ever volunteered an answer in class. Sat there as if she was totally unaware of what was going on around her and yet, when you stuck her with a question, even a difficult one, she'd stare at you with those strange brown eyes of hers until you were about to scold her for not paying attention and then she'd come up with the answer. The right answer. Once, in social studies, it was even an answer Miss Lundgren was sure they hadn't studied yet. Part of the material in the *Teacher's Guidebook* that she had been reading to give to the class tomorrow.

It bothered her so much she mentioned the 'little Morgan girl' to Mr Gordon in the staff room at lunch. Old Man Gordon, as the children and even some of the teachers called him behind his back, had grown up and gone to school in the Hurry district himself. He probably knew more about the local family histories than most of the families knew themselves. 'If Old Man Gordon ever writes one of them district-history books that's so popular these days, it'll be a bestseller. Course he'll be run out of town!' went the comments. Sure enough Mr Gordon came up with some information.

'Julie Morgan's getting to you, eh? Sweet, quiet child, with the sad look broken occasionally by that dazzling smile? Oh, "she doth teach the torches to burn bright," our Juliet. There's been one or two comments by teachers before. They can't stand it when a child doesn't follow the pattern. Julie, I heard, doesn't study, doesn't *appear* to listen in class, and frankly doesn't seem to be all that smart —'

'Ah, Mr Gordon,' the unmistakable accents of Miss Marion Johnson, former grade two teacher now librarian, interrupted, 'but she *reads*. The child is an absolutely *voracious* reader, Miss Lundgren. I actually feel sorry for her. I'm sure she's read every book in that library, even the encyclopaedia. If she remembers even a tiny portion of what she's read —'

'You don't,' said Mr Gordon, leaning forward conspiratorially, 'hold with the possibility that the young Morgan wench has inherited some of old Granny Morgan's talents then, Miss Johnson?'

'If you're referring to Will Morgan's grand-mother, I've heard all about her. A primitive old lady who hardly spoke any English . . . superstitious, as everyone was in her day . . .'

'Went around witchin' wells. Couldn't be beat. She'd find water in the desert, they said.'

'Oh, a diviner.' Miss Lundgren felt more com-fortable. 'Like in Margaret Laurence's book. I'm sure there's a scientific explanation for the way they get those forked sticks to point to where there are underground streams. Probably some-thing magnetic . . . or something . . .'

'Something, indeed!' said Mr Gordon ominously.

'Nonsense, there's nothing superstitious about the Morgans. And Will is one of those salt-of-the-earth, basic people. I should know the Morgans. I've taught most of them. Will and two of his brothers, plus all of this younger generation. Except Julie.'

'Still, we've had some interesting old gals in this district, Miss Lundgren. There was even prim and proper Granny Goderich, passed on four or five years ago —'

'Mrs Goderich was a dear old lady who just read teacups to oblige the local folk, Miss Lundgren —'

'With uncanny accuracy.'

Miss Johnson set her coffee cup down with an abrupt unladylike clatter. 'I assume, Mr Gordon, that you are merely giving Miss Lundgren a sample of your quaint semi-literate sense of humour.'

'It's true the old Goderich girl fronted with tea-cups, but Granny Morgan came right out and admitted to my grandad once that she came from a long line of seers. Wasn't Will Morgan the seventh child?'

The bell rang and the staff room reluctantly began to empty.

'Ignore him, Miss Lundgren,' said Miss Johnson firmly as she left the room.

'Hmmm. Folk superstitions are not always to be sneezed at. Seventh child of a seventh child was always thought to have some power. Your young Juliet would qualify, I believe, Miss Lundgren? Hmmm.' Mr Gordon walked down the hallway chuckling.

When Miss Lundgren made her take the ship book back, Julie wasn't too disappointed. She'd seen all she wanted to see. She was sure if there was something there that explained the ships to her she would have known where to look.

The library was deserted when she got there except for Miss Johnson who was unpacking some books.

'Ah, Juliet! Coming to get another book already?'

'Miss Lundgren says this is a picture book and I shouldn't have it. I'm supposed to be reading.'

Julie placed the book carefully on the return shelf.

'I know you've read just about everything we have. Perhaps there's something in this new box. The county's cut our book budget again and . . .,' Miss Johnson's glasses slid down her nose and fell into the box.

'Is there anything about ships? Sailing ships . . . like in the old days?'

'My goodness! Ships?' Miss Johnson paused in her search. 'Whatever do you want to know about ships for?'

'Old-days ships, Miss Johnson . . . because . . .'

Miss Johnson was busily stacking books beside her on the long library table; her glasses seemed to have disappeared in the box of packing. Perhaps, Julie thought, I don't have to have a reason. She might forget.

But she didn't. She was looking at Julie curiously. Sometimes, for all her fussiness and dither, Miss Johnson could give you a sharp look as if she really knew what was going on.

'Don't underestimate Miss Johnson,' her father used to scold the boys when they made fun of Miss Johnson's Library Time is Quiet Time or Be Nice to Our Friends, the Books. 'She used to be one of my favourite teachers. Knows a lot that woman. Right in the middle of some dull subject she'd come up with some little-known fact that wasn't in the books but kind of made you stop and think. Sort of put a new light on the subject.'

She was still looking at Julie.

'. . . because . . . because they were beautiful, I guess.'

'Why yes, Julie,' she seemed pleased. 'It must have been a wonderful sight to stand on the shore and see those ships, their masts to the wind . . . or away from it. . . . I'd have to check that.' She fished her glasses out of the strips of paper packing in the bottom of the box and put them on.

'I'm afraid the only thing that might interest you is this one, *The Voyages of Captain Cook.* He did travel in sailing ships.'

Julie nodded. She could see the book as Miss Johnson flipped through it. There were some pictures of the right kind of ships but it was mostly writing so it ought to satisfy Miss Lundgren. 'I'd like that one please, Miss Johnson.'

She waited patiently while Miss Johnson checked off her list, glued the little envelope on the back, and wondered where her stamp pad had got to.

Through the library window she could see the fluffy clouds drifting along the treetops but even when she squinted her eyes they did not turn into ships, although one looked a little bit like a squirrel with his tail arched over his back. No, her ships had been real. She sighed.

'I'm sorry to keep you so long.' Miss Johnson was all efficiency now, stamping the book and Julie's card.

Julie wondered if she ought to tell Miss Johnson

that a piece of the packing strips had stuck with her glasses and was hanging beside her ear like tinsel on a Christmas tree.

'Did you know,' said Miss Johnson as Julie was going out the door, 'that when the natives in the South Seas first saw Captain Cook's ships they ignored them because they knew such things could not exist!'

Julie shut the door quickly and leaned her face against it. She felt numb. She was glad that Miss Johnson hadn't dropped that 'little-known fact' while they were face to face. Glad too that there was nobody in the hall when she turned and began to walk slowly back to her classroom.

CHAPTER FOURTEEN

'Dad — '

'Don't talk with your mouth full, Billy,' said their mother absently, noticing that Julie had hardly touched her supper again.

'Dad,' said Billy carefully, 'what's a seer?'

'A steer? You know very well, Billy Morgan,' hooted Joe.

'No, a seer. Tommy Behan was listenin' outside the staff room at noon and he heard Old Man Gordon sayin' that your Granny Morgan told *his* grandad that she came from a long line of seers.'

'Gilbert Gordon is a gossip,' said their mother.

'*Gil*bert . . . *Gil*bert!' Jane wiggled with delight. 'Is that Old Man Gordon's name? *Gil*bert?'

'Never mind, Jane.' Their mother began clearing plates from the table. 'He's *Mister* Gordon to you. Whose turn is it to help?'

'I'm not finished yet, Mum.'

'But, what is it, Dad?'

'It's somebody who sees things that are going to happen, before they happen,' announced Jimmy. 'The ancient Romans called them soothsayers. They read entrails or something.'

'Yuck!' Jane pushed her plate away. 'You do pick great things to talk about at the table. How can you *read* entrails, anyway, that's dumb.'

'Like this.' Joe picked up a strand of Jane's hair and held it out, feigning disgust. 'I see by these entrails that this chicken is dead!'

'Mum! Tell Joe to stop being such a jerk!'

'Did Great-Granny Morgan read entrails, Dad?'

'Good heavens no, Billy. Joe, stop being silly. Is it your turn to help?'

'Dad?'

'No, Billy, not that I ever heard of. But people used to think some people could predict the future. And I guess once or twice your great-grandmother Morgan came surprisingly close.'

'Like that lady who told her friend not to take a certain aeroplane and he did and it crashed?' volunteered Jane.

'Something like that.'

'Will, don't fill the children's heads with those old family superstitions. It's Tuesday. Who's down for Tuesday? If I have to go look on the job list, it'll go hard for someone.'

'It's *my* turn, Mum, but I'm not *finished*.' Joe busied himself buttering another slice of bread. 'That's kind of like the story Mrs Behan told us about Granny Goderich. Said she knew there was going to be a train crash, but Old Man Goderich wouldn't listen and —'

'*Mister* Goderich, Joey. You children get worse every day.'

'Mister Goderich sent young George on that trip anyhow and he got killed. She never forgave him, Mrs Behan said.'

'You children shouldn't listen to gossip like that.

Of course people sometimes have a feeling something will happen. If it doesn't, they forget, but if it does everyone gets excited and thinks —'

'That'd be awful,' breathed Jane, 'knowing and not being able to do anything . . .'

Julie pushed back her chair, her face white.

'You sick, Punkin?' Her father was up and lifting her, her face buried in his shoulder. 'Thought you were off your feed,' he said as he carried her upstairs.

'She's had all her shots,' said Jimmy looking hard at Jane.

Her father put Julie down as gently as he could and piled up the pillows. 'People are funny,' he shook his head as he pulled up Julie's old quilt. 'One time they'll believe something, then it goes out of style and it's either considered stupid or sinful.'

Julie's eyes rested on the quilt patch from her great-grandmother's wedding gown. The blue was faded and worn thin from the years and Julie's rubbing — just a shadow of the blue the spring bride had worn. Tonight she was afraid to touch the patch at first but finally she held it to her cheek.

She noticed the satin was wet. It frightened her a moment and then she realized that both her cheeks were wet. She'd been crying. Stupid! Now she couldn't even recognize tears, real tears, her own tears.

I'm just like those South Sea islanders. Don't know what's real and what isn't. Except the islanders ignored what they saw if it was something they knew shouldn't be in their world. That was a mistake. So what is real? Who can know?

Still holding the quilt patch Julie wriggled down under the covers and closed her eyes. She needed the comfort of the smiling brown eyes tonight, she felt so alone. Then just before she slipped into sleep it happened. There was the crowd of people, and the young woman in the vibrant blue dress laughing in the spring sunshine. But this time when she turned toward Julie her smile faded. She stared straight at Julie and her eyes were frightened like those of a trapped wild thing.

CHAPTER FIFTEEN

Julie woke up in a tangle of quilt and pillows with
the sun streaming in the window and her mother
standing beside her bed.

'Are you feeling better now, Julie?' Her mother's hand went automatically to Julie's forehead.

'I'm okay, Mum. Where is everybody? Did I
miss the school bus?'

'Your father thought you should stay home
today. He thought maybe you were coming
down with something. No fever, though. You
sure you feel better?'

'Sure, Mum.' Julie untangled herself from the
bedclothes and started hunting for clean socks.

'Anything special you'd like for breakfast . . .
poached eggs on toast? You haven't been eating
much the last couple of days.'

'Just the usual.' Jane had taken her favourite
blue knee highs again and left Julie the ones with
the holes. She'd have to go dig in the odd-sock
basket by the washing machine and see if she
could find a pair that matched.

'How am I going to get to school? I'm not
really sick.' Julie had finished most of her egg
and was looking under the band-aid on her arm
to see if the scab had fallen off yet. She hoped

her mother would tell her to stay home but she didn't feel like spending the day in bed.

'Your father said he'd drive you if you felt better after lunch. He's gone to bring the tractor back from Behan's. Why don't you feed the chickens for me? I'd like to get started on the housework.'

It was a relief to get outside. Julie realized that it must have poured during the night. The water still stood in puddles in the yard and the roofs of the buildings steamed in the morning sunlight. She took deep gulps of breath trying to relieve the heavy feeling she felt in her chest. It was a strange feeling but she knew she wasn't sick. It was something else.

She finished mixing the mash for the hens, scattered some grain for Billy's banties, and headed back to the house. She'd forgotten the egg pail and she might as well gather eggs now before they got broken in the nests. Her mother always made the person who did the chickens that day wash the eggs at night. If you gathered them often, there weren't many that needed cleaning.

Then she saw it.

Right over the summerfallow field, where she'd seen the others. But this time there was only one and this time she knew right away what it was because she'd seen one like it in the ship book. The Egyptian Ship of the Dead, the caption had said. It was moving very slowly, the sails not even appearing to be caught in the wind; the front and back parts caught up like a narrow basket, like the pea-pod boats she and Billy used to make.

It floated toward her above the wet black dirt of the field. Her chest hurt as if she couldn't get her breath in fast enough, as if she could not breathe at all.

And then came the smell. The familiar, beloved smell of her father's workshirt, and she began to run. Blindly, and in terror of what she knew and what she did not want to know.

Even as she ran, Julie knew that it was wrong, that she must not do it. It was too far and there was too little time for her to run there.

She slowed down as she was nearing the corral and heard rather than saw Diablo snort and rear nearby.

Her father's latest stallion was a beauty. Black, with enough Arab blood to give him a fine head and fiery disposition, he was big enough to make him popular with the quarter-horse owners who wanted to liven up their stock. They hadn't had him long and so far nobody'd been able to make friends with him, not even Julie.

She didn't stop to try. Friendship was the last thing she cared about just now. She was up the corral railing and on his back before he could move away.

He moved fast enough then. Did not buck but hurled himself the length of the corral straight for the far fence. Julie clung to the mane. Leaned along the great neck, eyes shut tight, felt the shoulder muscles tense, lift, soar. She waited for the jolt, the twist, the inevitable plunge when his hooves caught on the rails. It didn't happen.

Headlong they raced. Down the driveway out to the main road, north toward Behan's.

Julie could not slow or turn him. She would not have wanted to. And all the time the fear enfolded her. It was not of the ride. It was separate from the plunging animal to whose back she clung. Not really fear, either. Dread. Dread of what she would find when she arrived, and she did not know when she would arrive or why she was going.

The wind made her eyes water and she closed them again. Closed them and pressed close to the stallion's neck as he raced along. Diablo surged forward as though impelled by her urgency, as though sharing her terror.

There were no cars and the horse with its clinging burden took the centre of the dirt road.

Julie would never know how long it took before they topped the hill near Behan's and she saw it. Moments . . . years. And she knew before she could distinguish what it was or even recognize the green tractor that her father lay underneath it by the washout of the sandhill.

Diablo did not, could not, stop. He swerved, slowing a little, changing direction, shying suddenly, and Julie jumped or was thrown or floated free — she could never be quite sure — landing against the sandbank, rolling, coming to a stop only inches from the man whose body was pinned under the tractor wheel. She opened her eyes winded but unhurt and stared directly into her father's face. It was blue and he didn't seem to be breathing.

CHAPTER SIXTEEN

Alice Morgan had planned to finish washing the living room walls that morning. She wanted to get one more wall done before eleven and she hadn't even started it yet. Instead, she'd been spending her time picking up glass and trying to patch together the old portrait she'd dropped.

It's not even worth salvaging, she thought. It's just that Will was fond of it. 'That picture of the lady clutching the book,' Jane called it. Except for the frame, which was one of those ornate gilt ones popular at the turn of the century and now much in demand in antique shops, she couldn't see that it had any value at all. It wasn't even a portrait of anyone in the family she was sure. There were dozens like it — almost every homestead had one; this one just had a nicer frame. She sighed. No time to start washing now. She'd better get on with dinner.

She was just adding water to the potatoes when she noticed the movement in the corral. Diablo was lively today. She often stood here by the sink and watched him trot back and forth along the fence, arching his neck and calling to the mares. He'd moved behind the granaries now and she was about to turn away when she saw them. At first she didn't see Julie on his back, only that he was going dead out and heading straight for the fence. That was bad enough. Then she realized — recognized the slight figure crouching along his neck. Julie! Why? What on earth had possessed the girl? She never rode anymore. She had not done so for years. Not since she was little.

To her mother it seemed like a bad dream. Once again she was standing at the window, frozen with fear just as she had been all those years ago. But this time she was alone. There was no Will to take charge, walk across the yard, and lift Julie down. And this time the horse was not behaving like some gentle giant. This time he was galloping, charging like a mad thing straight for the rail fence.

Terrified. She stood staring even as her mind willed her to rush to the door and run out to be there for the inevitable disaster. She saw what Julie felt: the big horse pause, tense, and begin his jump.

'He can't possibly . . .' Alice sobbed, and moved at last. Rushed across the kitchen and flung open the door. In time to see them land and, without seeming to decrease speed, race across the yard and down the lane to the road.

She waited only long enough to see them turn north on the main road and then she began to run. She was amazed that she was thinking clearly in spite of her panic. Her mind was carefully clicking along while her body ran.

The keys to the car were back in the house in her purse, she knew; anyway she would have to waste time opening the garage door. Instead, she ran for the old truck. Will usually left the keys in it. Yes. There they were.

For once it started immediately. Alice gave it only a moment and then threw it into gear. She wrestled the steering wheel trying to turn sharply enough to swing out of the yard without having to stop, change gears, and back up. She narrowly missed the gatepost and then fought the steering wheel back, straightening the truck with a jerk. Then she pushed the gas pedal to the floor.

Judging by the mad look in Diablo's eyes, Alice thought, he would run until he dropped. Or something hit him.

'Don't let any trucks be on the road,' she prayed.

Why had Julie done anything so foolish? Even as she asked herself, she knew that it was not like Julie to be foolish, that she must have had a very good reason. With terrible clarity she knew that Will had not told her the truth about Granny Goderich that night. She feared Julie's reason now.

It took Julie a moment to get her wind back. She lay still gasping. But inside she was calm and sure. She knew what she had to do.

In the moments before her father lost consciousness he had been able to work his legs loose. Now he lay pinned across the chest by the edge of the tractor tyre. Julie could see where he had tried to dig himself out — useless scrapings with his hands. Still, digging was the only way: she couldn't move the tractor.

She grabbed a broken bit of board that lay nearby

114

and began digging. Carefully. The soft sand came away easily. She'd loosen a bit with the board, then scoop it out with her hands. Quickly. Efficiently.

She didn't stop when the truck pulled up, only looked up for a moment and called, 'Bring the shovel out of the back, Mum!'

Her mother did. And seeing Will's face, his lips blue and motionless, she began to cry.

'Hold his head up, Mum, while I dig.' Julie snatched the shovel from her and began to dig, scooping out what was almost a tunnel under his back and shoulders.

'Stop crying, Mum! You've got to blow in his mouth. Remember, you said you took a lifesaving course once in Girl Guides. Blow in his mouth. Now.'

Alice realized that more of Will's weight was on her: the wheel was not crushing his chest as much. Julie's tunnel had released some of the pressure. She bent, put her lips to his, and blew. Trying to hold back the sobs and do it evenly the way she vaguely recalled the instructor telling them to do it. Once. Twice. Was she doing it too fast? Wasn't she supposed to be counting? She couldn't remember. She waited, tense and breathless herself. Beside her she was aware of Julie, still scooping the sand away.

'We might be able to pull him out a little in a minute.' Julie looked up. 'Don't stop! Blow again, Mum.'

Alice bent and as she did she felt the exhaled breath, the small convulsive moan. 'Julie! He's

115

breathing!' Again a shallow gasp. The chest moving slightly. She was sure now.

'Put your arms around him and see if you can pull him down and out. Try, Mum.'

Alice obeyed. It wasn't hard. It was a fairly steep slope and the sand slid along, making it easier. A few more inches and she'd have him out from under the tractor.

'Look, Julie,' she sobbed with relief. 'He's breathing . . . and he's almost out from under. Just grab his legs and help me — Julie!' She turned toward her daughter and then stopped. Julie was standing motionless, staring at the tractor. Her face white, expressionless as if she were far away or under some sort of hypnotic spell. Alice knew she could not hear, could not move.

Oh no, she thought, now Julie's in shock and there's nobody to help. She began to pull frantically. She realized that she would never be able to get Will into the truck alone, even with Julie's help. He was out from under the tractor. He was breathing. She would have to leave Julie with him and drive for help. And Julie . . .

Alice didn't even realize Paddy Behan was there until he began to help her, carefully lifting Will and moving past the still, motionless Julie toward the truck.

'God, Alice, it's a good thing I happened along. I was just turnin' into the yard and I spotted the truck. Didn't think nothin' of it 'til I saw the tractor and then you. Don't worry now. He's hurt bad, but he's breathin'. We'll get him into the hospital. Here,

116

get that tailgate down and throw that blanket into the back. How'd you ever get him out from under there all by yourself, anyway?'

'Julie helped . . .,' she began. Spreading the blanket she could look over the side of the truck box and see Julie, her eyes still fixed on the tractor. As her mother watched Julie turned and behind her the tractor began to move, to roll the rest of the way, laying at last on its side in the ditch. The handle of the shovel poked out from under the huge rear wheel.

At Alice's gasp, Behan turned. 'Dammit,' he breathed, 'if Will ain't a lucky man you come along when you did!'

Julie did not turn to look behind her. Her face was still white, drained of colour. As Alice watched, Julie's legs gave way and she crumpled like a rag doll.

'Poor kid. Been a big shock for her. She'll be okay.' Paddy stripped off his denim jacket and covered Will. 'You okay to ride in the back?'

'Yes, I'm fine . . .' Alice was lifting Julie, who clung limply to her as they moved to the truck. She half pushed, half lifted her daughter into the cab.

'. . . not going to be the best ride to town but it's faster than calling an ambulance. I'll stop by the house and get Mary to phone Doc Barnes; maybe he can meet us at the hospital.'

Alice lay down on the blanket beside Will. She wanted to warm him, to shelter him with her body but she was afraid to touch him. Afraid to do anything to his injured chest. Still she could not take her eyes from his face, willing each breath to happen. Trying not to notice the trickle of blood at the side of his mouth. She was suddenly aware of how hot the sun was. She'd been grateful before because she knew the patient should be kept warm, but now she was afraid of the heat pounding against that pale, almost waxen face and she raised her head to shelter him.

She could see Julie slumped on the front seat not moving. She no longer questioned or cared how Julie knew when she was needed. Granny Goderich. Aunt Em. It really didn't matter. Poor Julie. They'd all been hard on her but Alice knew that she had been the worst. Rejecting, fearing her own daughter.

And now this business with the tractor. Alice trembled, remembering the way it had begun to move when Julie took her eyes away from it. Suddenly rolling down the slope as if the prop that had held it had been taken away. It was something more than the 'second sight' Will talked of in his grandmother. How had Julie done it? Worse still, did she *know*? How frightening for Julie to be wrestling with this strange knowledge . . . and be so alone.

Alice noticed Behan's anxious glance. She tried to smile to signal that the breathing was continuing. She was afraid he would read her expression the wrong way and stop the truck.

They were at Behan's house now. Had that only been a quarter of a mile? Still five miles to go. It was taking too long. She was aware of the screen door slamming as Behan rushed in. And again, as Mary rushed out carrying blankets and a pillow for Will.

Alice was grateful to Mary Behan for her calm, matter-of-fact silence. No questions. No useless suggestions. She reached over the truck box and took her hand and held it quietly, steadily. Only when Paddy returned to the truck to announce that Doc Barnes would be waiting at Emergency did she speak.

'Do you want to leave Julie here?' Her eyes were on the motionless girl in the front seat.

'No!' Alice's voice was involuntarily sharp, frightened. 'I need her! I mean . . . I want her . . . I need to talk to her . . . I'm . . .'

She could see Julie straighten a little. Turn and try to smile. A small, sad smile. Alice tried to smile back but couldn't. The sad smile was almost harder to bear than the limp despair Julie had shown before. What did it mean Alice wondered?

CHAPTER SEVENTEEN

It was not until the truck pulled into the emergency entrance of the hospital that Julie was able to think again. The green weight of the tractor that had dominated her thoughts lifted. She felt very tired and, more than ever, confused.

The mad ride, she could understand; it was the same force that had called her to Granny Goderich. The frantic digging was, after all, the only thing to do, although someone else might have wondered that she had known so precisely the right way to go about it. But the tractor? When had she known its menace? Not during the digging surely. Had it moved as her mother began to pull her father free? Julie couldn't remember. Only remembered the compulsion to stare at the tractor until it seemed to be the only thing in the world . . . in the universe . . . in her mind.

She sighed and stepped out of the truck. Someone, Mr Behan perhaps, had opened the door and then rushed away.

There was a group of people around her father, moving him onto a stretcher. She recognized Dr Barnes. Saw him talking to her mother and caught the words 'ambulance . . . Red Deer . . . may have to operate . . .' Everyone moved away following the stretcher.

Julie leaned on the truck, taking deep breaths. Was she going to be sick? She wasn't dizzy. Just that she'd never felt so empty before ... vacant ... or flat. That was how she felt. As if a breeze could pick her up and waft her away like a torn piece of paper.

'Come on, Julie. Are you all right?' Behan's voice was concerned. She realized that her mother was there and Dr Barnes.

'Poor Julie.' Dr Barnes's arm was around her, strong and supporting. 'It's been too much for you. Mr Behan will drive you home.'

'Mum?' Julie wasn't sure what she should do. Was there anything she could do now?

'It's all right, Julie. Mrs Behan will be there and she'll give you kids supper. Dr Barnes is going to come in the ambulance with Daddy to Red Deer.' Her mother hugged her tightly. 'I'll phone you.' She turned away then paused, turned, and held Julie close again. 'Oh Julie,' she whispered as if it was very hard to say, '. . . I love you.'

Julie and Mr Behan got to the farm just after the school bus. Mrs Behan was there in the kitchen with a plateful of sandwiches. She was handing out mugs of soup — the boys would be late doing chores tonight.

The words flew in her face as she came in the door.

'You got there first, Julie! ... wasn't breathing ... How'd you dig him out? ... We saw the tractor from the school bus ... Hey, Mr Outram just phoned, Diablo's over at his place. That's five

121

miles from here. How'd he get there? . . . Was Dad okay? . . . Is he going to be okay? . . . When's Mum going to phone? . . .

This time Julie knew she was going to be sick.

She stayed in the bathroom a long time running the water. The phone rang and she could hear Mrs Behan telling the others that they were going to have to operate to take the fragments of broken ribs from his lungs. She slipped into the bedroom, took the dalmatian from her shelf, and ran out the back door.

In the darkening sky black clouds climbed from the horizon. The only white cloud in sight was the thunderhead balancing on top of the dark ones. But it was not the storm clouds that Julie saw, it was the reed ship with its black sails. And now she knew what it meant. The death ship.

She ran from it. Ran to her tree.

Breathless, Julie stood by the old tree as she had years before when she was afraid to start school. Weeping and afraid.

'What good is it?' she sobbed. 'What use is it to know what's going to happen if I can't help . . . can't use my knowledge to change things?'

The tree leaves rustled in understanding.

'Granny Goderich said the Times are different but the Gift isn't. She knew something was going to happen to George.' Julie rubbed the dalmatian against her cheek. Above her the branches rattled in the rising wind.

'What use is it, knowing he will die, if I can't help . . . can't *do* anything?'

The wind that shook the branches of the old tree bent and whipped the young poplars in the pasture beyond. Julie clung to the trunk, her face pressed to the rough bark. In the distance there was the rumble of thunder.

'Granny Goderich knew but she couldn't stop what happened to George.'

The wind was stronger now, buffeting her so that she could hardly stand. She clung to her tree; felt the bark change and soften against her cheek. She could hear Granny Goderich's voice, 'I let him go . . . I was too weak.'

Above her the old tree creaked and groaned, tormented by the wind. Julie dropped the dalmatian and backed away from the tree. The wind whipped her hair against her face now wet with tears but she didn't notice. The words 'I let him go' echoed inside her.

Her voice was lost in the noise, the wind. 'I won't let him die!' She felt again the weight of the tractor and knew that she was not weak. The Times were different but she was different too. And she was strong. 'He *won't* die!' she cried, her words swept from her by the wind.

A great moan came from the old tree as it fell.

Alice Morgan sat alone in the surgery waiting room. She had phoned home as soon as they'd arrived in Red Deer. Now there was nothing to do but wait. And hope. She wished Julie were with her. She looked up as Dr. Barnes and the surgeon came out.

'He's all right, Alice.' Dr. Barnes came over and took her hand. 'I don't mind telling you it was close, though. His heart stopped on the table. . . . Strangest thing, we couldn't seem to get it going for a minute and then suddenly it started beating again on its own . . . strong as ever.' He put his arm around her shaking shoulders. 'Don't worry, he'll be all right now. Will's as strong as an ox, he'll make a quick recovery. As soon as the anaesthetic wears off you'll be able to talk to him.'

In the pasture, the wind was now just a breeze stirring Julie's tangled hair as she began to walk home. Behind her, under the mangled and broken branches of the fallen tree lay a shattered china dog. Above, black storm clouds moved westward and, riding after the storm, brilliant white thunderheads formed against the vivid blue sky. Clouds, white and billowing, like the sails of great ships, dazzling in the light of the returning sun and Julie's smile.

Other Kelpies by the same author:

The Doll

If you liked this book then why not
look out for other Kelpies. There are
more than fifty titles to choose from
and they are available from all good bookshops.

For a free Kelpie badge, catalogue and
any other information, please send
a stamped addressed envelope to:
Margaret Ritchie (K.C.B.)
Canongate Publishing Ltd.,
16 Frederick Street, Edinburgh EH2 2HB